Racing To Find An Assassin

Max Porter

This is a work of fiction. Names, characters, places, and incidents are either the product of the author's imagination or are used fictitiously. Any resemblance to actual persons, living or dead, businesses, companies, events, or locales is entirely coincidental.

Cover photograph is by Sheena Clauson

Also written by Max Porter
Odyssey of a Horseman

Copyright © 2011 Max Porter
All rights reserved.

ISBN: 1-4610-3225-3
ISBN-13: 9781461032250

I was sitting in the first row of box seats in the grandstand, watching three of my horses work an easy half-mile. I spend a lot of my time here in the mornings because I have always insisted on watching my horses on the track. The exercise rider will come back and tell you the horse went fine, even if he had been a complete idiot. Riders seem to think if a horse acts up you will blame them for it.

A horse acts up on the track for a lot of reasons, and it isn't always the riders fault. What I am most interested in is how fast the horse went, and you can't ever take a riders word for that. I have had riders tell me the horse went great, when in fact, he ran away for a mile or more. If a trainer doesn't know how far and how fast his horse goes every day, he is at a disadvantage in trying to fine-tune the horse's conditioning.

My regular riders know that I watch every horse, and they don't try telling me what they think I want to hear. The exercise riders at most tracks tend to be a little unreliable, and very often you must use whoever is available. These are the riders that remind you why you watch every horse.

2

I had just hit the stop button on my watch as the horses crossed the wire when the loudspeaker announced that I had visitors at the stable gate. They were going to have to wait for a few minutes. I wasn't expecting anyone and I wasn't going to leave until my horses pulled up and left the track. I jotted down the times in my notebook and watched the set pull up. They all came back levelheaded and headed for the barn before I left my seat and went to the stable gate.

As I walked to the gate, I assumed this was a nuisance call and was impatiently thinking about the things I needed to be doing at the barn. My owners were all licensed and didn't need me to get through the gate. At this time of day, it probably was a groom or exercise rider that had just hit town and wanted me to sign him into the stable area so he could look for a job.

I was surprised to see two well-dressed gentlemen standing patiently awaiting my arrival. They were so similar that I first thought they might be brothers, but as I got closer, I didn't see any facial resemblance. They wore suits and ties, and both stood an inch or two over six feet. They were clean shaven and had expensive haircuts. No barber shop quickies here. These boys used stylists. I judged them to be late thirties, but they were in such good physical shape they might be a little older.

As I approached the gate, the stable guard must have told them who I was, because they came over to meet me. The first man to reach me held out his hand and introduced himself.

"Mr. Holden, my name is Robert Goodman and this is my friend William St. Germaine."

I shook both of their hands and said, "Just call me Chance. There's no need for the mister. What can I do for you?"

Goodman assumed the role of spokesman and said, "We are interested in owning a racehorse or two, and several people have told us the first step is to find a trainer. I was hoping that when you have time you could sit down with us and discuss it."

This didn't sound very promising. I don't like to take on new owners. They don't know anything about the business, and they come in with their expectations too high. After they have been around two or three months, they think they have learned enough to start giving you advice on the training of their horse. Very often they become such a nuisance you have to suggest they find another trainer, and they leave with bad feelings. After a couple years of experience, they may turn into good owners that you would enjoy having, but that bridge has been burned.

I would at least give them some conversation and maybe a little free advice if I liked them. I said, "I have an hour or two of work left at the barn. You can come over and hang around or you can go over to the kitchen and I'll meet you there as soon as I am finished."

Goodman looked blank and said, "The kitchen?"

"On the racetrack the horseman's cafeteria is called the kitchen. It also serves as sort of a horseman's lounge; people will be there playing cards or just sitting around passing the track gossip. You might find it interesting."

Goodman thought it over for a minute before he said, "You know what. I like gossip. If you can give us directions, we'll wait for you there. We don't want to interfere with your work."

I would pass right by the kitchen on the way to the barn so I walked them over. "Just go on in and get a cup of coffee and hang out. There will be several people sitting around killing time; you won't feel out of place."

Walking back to the barn, I tried to decide what was going on here. It didn't feel right. Most newcomers would have jumped at the chance to hang around the shed row during training. It was possible they were afraid of getting their suits dirty, but you would think they should at least be curious enough to take a look.

4

The work at the barn was winding down when I got back and there wasn't much left to do. I checked a few legs and questioned a couple of the grooms about horses in their care that had problems. Most of my time was spent going over each horse's training schedule, making decisions about what they needed to do tomorrow, and when they would race. I was finished in about an hour.

I didn't have any horses racing today so I could give these guys a couple of hours without being pressed for time. If they had come tomorrow when I had three in, they would have been out of luck. I walked over to the kitchen going over some of the questions I needed answers for before I would consider having them as clients.

The first question was very important. Could they afford it? Lawrence J Peters and Raymond Hull's book *The Peter Principle* states that "everyone rises to the level of their incompetence." The racetrack is a prime example of this thought. If an owner can afford one horse, he has three. If he can afford five, he has ten. They always seem to rise to the number just out of their ability to carry, and it puts trainers in the position of always trying to collect training bills. I hate that part of the business, but you can't train a horse without being paid. The really bad part is the longer they are with you and the better friends they become the more they expect you to carry on your books without complaining. They don't seem to understand that the payroll has to be met every week and that feed bills, vet bills, etcetera must be paid in a timely manner. Training horses is an expensive proposition and the bills are never ending.

I walked into the kitchen expecting to find the guys sitting in a corner watching people. Instead Goodman was in a card game and St. Germaine was sitting at a table talking with two exercise riders. My first thought was, if this was their first time at a racetrack, how come Goodman knew how to play racehorse.

Racehorse is a rummy game similar to Tonk that is played at every racetrack in America, but I have never seen it played other than at a racetrack. It is played all day everyday in nearly every racetrack kitchen in the country and can become very addictive. I recall a trainer playing in our game one day. He had the West Coast string for a big owner from Florida. The game had started about eleven o'clock and at about three, one of his grooms came over to tell him that they were getting ready to take the horse over for his race and that the owner was wondering where he was. We had just started a new game and he told the groom he would be over in about fifteen minutes.

One of the players said, "You must be kidding. Your owner is here from Florida for this race, and you're here playing cards?"

The reply was just a shrug and the game went on. He didn't go over for the race and continued to play until the game broke up about five. I was not very surprised when an article appeared in The Form about a month later stating that the string had been given to another trainer. The card player now grubs out a living as an overweight exercise rider.

I recall a note hung on the bulletin board one day that read, "Groom wanted." It went on to say that the applicant must not be a racehorse player and even listed by name a groom that played every day as a person that need not apply. I thought it was humorous but at the same time a little sad that these guys screwed up their lives over a card game.

I walked over to see how Goodman was doing in the game and heard him announce that his trainer was here, so this would be his last game. I watched the last couple of hands and saw that he was a competent player and was holding his own. When the game was over, he owed only twelve dollars, and paid off before getting up from the table. Two of the players in the game were very good players, so for him to only lose twelve dollars indicated that he had played very well.

I bought a soft drink and seated us at a table far enough from everyone to have a little privacy. He and I sat down, and in about five minutes, St. Germaine joined us.

"Where did you learn to play racehorse?" I asked.

"I have never played before, but after watching the game for about half an hour, I could see that it was just rummy with fewer starting cards. I have also played Tonk a few times, which is a very similar game. When one of the players quit, I asked if I could take his place. I like the game. Do they play every day?"

"They play all day, every day. Now what kind of information can I give you fellows?"

Since Goodman again assumed the role of spokesman, I had to think that he was the senior partner of this pair. Or at least it was his idea, and St. Germaine was just going along.

"We are interested in getting a horse or two, and we need to know just basic information. We would like to have some idea what it will cost to purchase and maintain a decent horse."

"The term 'decent horse' has a lot of leeway. A decent horse to me means a horse that can win at whatever level you are running him. But those levels stretch from a ten thousand dollar claiming horse to stakes horses, with a lot of steps in between. You must give me some idea of where you want to fall in that range."

"We don't even know what those steps are. What range would you recommend for a couple of guys making their first try at horseracing?"

"If you want to be racing right away, you will need to claim a horse that is already racing. To start with an unraced baby is a time-consuming process, and newcomers get bored with the whole thing before their horse ever gets to the races. Many times an injury prevents the horse from ever reaching the races, and your investment is a total loss. If you are going to claim a horse, I suggest you don't take one from the bottom. If you claim a horse at the bottom and he is not as good as you hoped for, you have no place to go with him. If you claim a horse for thirty thousand and he turns out to be subpar, you might still make your money back running for less. I don't like claiming a horse at the bottom and almost never do it."

"If we claimed a thirty thousand dollar horse, what would be our expenses to keep him racing?"

"You can expect to have bills in the two or three thousand dollars per month range, depending on cost from vet bills. If the horse has problems, you will probably be at the top of that range. If you are lucky enough to make a good claim, the horse should pay for himself and even make a profit. It is rare to have a total loss of investment, but it can happen."

"How do we go about choosing which horse to claim?"

"A claim must be agreeable to all parties. From time to time, I see a horse that I like for the price he is running, and I can make a suggestion you take him. If you don't like him for some reason, we don't claim him. You might be following a horse that you like and suggest we claim him. If I don't like him for some reason, I will not take him for you. You can always get another trainer to claim him for you, but if I think he is a bad claim, I can't be pressured into claiming him against my will. Claiming is a judgment call, and you can't have finger pointing afterwards if it doesn't work out well."

"How do we make a claim?"

"You must get an owners license, and you must deposit the money with the horseman's bookkeeper before you make a claim.

Once you drop your claim in the box, unless there are multiple claims on the same horse, you own the horse at the end of the race even if it drops dead during the race. In the case of multiple claims for the same horse, you draw lots after the race. Whoever wins the draw is then the owner."

"You think this is the best way to enter racing?"

"For a newcomer it is the only way to enter racing. The only thing that I emphasize is to do your homework in choosing a reliable trainer. Like the brokerage business or any other business that deals in other people's money, the players are not all equal. There are a lot of hustlers out there, and they are not the only danger. One of the most costly things in this business is a trainer who represents himself as more knowledgeable than he actually is. There are many trainers in this business that I wouldn't allow to use my money to buy a bale of hay, but they have invested hundreds of thousands of dollars for owners. In some cases it is almost criminal, but there is nothing to be done about it. This is a business where there should be a large sign at the gate reminding you of the old adage, "Buyer Beware."

"If we decide to go ahead with this, what do we need to get a license?

"Because you don't already own a horse, you will need to get an approval from the stewards for a temporary license and their permission to make a claim."

Goodman extended his hand and said, "You have been a big help. I think that is all of the information we need today. We will most likely be going ahead with this and we'll be in touch soon."

"Would you mind if I asked why you came to me?"

They exchanged a strange look before Goodman said, "You came highly recommended by a friend of ours."

That was too vague for me and I said, "And that would be?"

"He didn't ask us to not mention his name, so I guess it's alright to tell you, it was James Wadell."

I pride myself on having a good poker face and not wearing my emotions on my sleeve, but it took a huge effort to hide my surprise. To cover any lapse in the conversation, I dug two of my business cards out and handed one to each of them.

As I stood up I said, "The number on the card is my cell phone, so you can reach me anytime. The road in front of the kitchen is the main road back to the gate where you came in, so you should have no trouble going back. It was nice to meet you both."

They both said their goodbyes and walked out while I sat back down to think this over. James Wadell was the uncle of my ex-wife. My ex and I had parted on terms as friendly as a divorce could be and were still sort of friends. The breakup was inevitable due to my life style. I am on the road a lot shipping from track to track, and sometimes I am gone for a month or two. I am an Oscar Wilde kind of guy, who can resist anything except temptation, and she finally had enough of my failures to resist.

I had only met James a couple of times during the five years we were married, and I wasn't sure I would recognize him if I ran into him on the street. The fact that I was divorced from his niece was not what had made his recommendation a shock. It was the fact that he was a career FBI man—and these guys knew him. I had felt at first meeting that something was wrong with this picture, and now there was no doubt in my mind. What could the FBI possibly find of interest about me?

I slowly went through my owners one by one, trying to find one that might warrant an FBI investigation. The best I could come up with was two of them that I had always thought were living above their means. After thinking it over, I had to admit that neither one lived so far above his means that it would draw the attention of the feds. There had to be another explanation.

Natural human guilt made me examine my life in minute detail. Had I associated with someone recently who might be of interest to the feds? I couldn't think of a single person that I had spoken to in years that had even had a run in with the local law, unless it would be some groom that had been pulled in for public intoxication. I didn't think that would have much interest for the FBI. I was fairly sure they weren't investigating me personally or they wouldn't have given me Wadell's name. I was at a total loss and would wait to see what developed. Who knows, I might never see them again.

I was in my car on the way to my apartment when a wild thought hit me. The background checks the racing board runs on applicants for a license as well as a lot of the investigations into illegal doping are done by the TRPB, which stands for Thoroughbred Racing Protective Bureau, which supposedly was, in the beginning, a branch of the FBI. If they were investigating me for the use of illegal drugs, they were going to be disappointed.

I have always maintained that any trainer who runs an unusually high win percentage has one of two things going on. He either has a blank check to buy anything he can't outrun or he is cheating. All racetracks are in a never-ending war with the cheaters. New drugs become available to the cheaters before the labs have a test for them, and many drugs can only be detected by a specific test. Each one of these tests is expensive enough to limit their use to the rare occasions when that particular drug is suspected. The cost of testing every horse for every drug known to man would bankrupt the world of racing.

When they do catch a trainer using drugs, the problem arises of what to do about it. If it is a straight up case, with penalties spelled out there is no problem. But when it is an exotic drug that took a long time to uncover, there can be serious implications.

A good example is a case that occurred a couple of years ago. We had a trainer right here that was running a decent win percentage of about sixteen percent. He had a big stable and ran a lot of horses. Suddenly his percentage went crazy and overnight jumped to thirty-five percent. He was claiming horses for twelve five, running them back for twenty and winning by daylight. For two months he had been winning races every day. It was rumored that the racing board was going crazy trying to pinpoint what he was running on.

I had some babies in training at Pomona, and had been over to check on them. I came back just about the time the races were starting, and a friend of mine stopped me at the gate. He asked if I was going to the races and cautioned me not to bet on any of this trainer's horses. The racetrack grapevine, which is pretty good, said the stewards had finally found what he was running on and had called him in. They told him they knew what it was, and if he used it again they would ban him for life. On this particular afternoon, he had five horses in, and they all ran up the track. Not one came close to even hitting the board.

At first glance it would appear that something was wrong with a no penalty call since the guy had stolen a lot of money. The magnitude of his theft was what saved him. When a winning horse is tested after the race; they take urine and blood samples. A portion of these samples is sent to the lab, and the remainder is frozen and stored. They do this because if the horse has a bad test, the trainer can ask for those samples to have an independent lab do another test. Since they have samples of all the winners this trainer has had during the meet, they would be obligated to go back and test them all for the exotic drug they had found him using. If they found a hundred horses that had to be disqualified the repercussions would be horrendous. Each race has four horses in the money plus the horse that just missed the money, and all of those purses would have to be readjusted and redistributed. The hundred owners who had received purse money on a disqualified horse would be more than unhappy, and many of them wouldn't return it without court action. Also, remember that many of those horses had multiple owners so that all of the owners involved would be tainted for the rest of their lives for taking part in a doping scandal even though most of them had no idea anything was going on. The process was so overwhelming that it was much better to sweep it under the rug and make sure it never happened again.

By the time I got home, I had thought through the meeting from start to finish. I still believed that if they were investigating me, they would never have given me Wadell's name. The only reasonable explanation was they were investigating someone stabled near me and needed an excuse to be around. There were several large stables around me, but there was no one that I could think of, who stood out as a possibility. If that's what this was about, they wouldn't go so far as investing the money to buy a horse. I might never see them again.

The next morning I was at my usual place in the grandstand watching my horses train. Santa Anita has a program that I think is great. They open the grandstand to the public in the morning. It allows the public to watch the horses train. Every horse that works is announced over the speaker system so the public knows which horse it is. They have a refreshment stand selling coffee and donuts and breakfast sandwiches. They even have a few mutual windows open for early betting. It allows a bettor to watch the horses train and make a wager before he goes to work. It is well received by the public, and I think all tracks should adopt this policy.

I had made my notes on the horse that had left the track and was waiting on the next horse when I noticed Goodman and St. Germaine at the refreshment stand. They were dressed in slacks and polo shirts—they must have realized that suits made them appear overdressed in this crowd.

They didn't seem to have any special agenda. With coffee in hand, they watched the horses on the track and moved around among the other watchers. They struck up a few idle conversations but didn't seem to be talking seriously to anyone. Most of the morning people seem to hang around down on the apron. I think they like being as close to the horses as possible.

They didn't spot me sitting up in the grandstand, and I didn't go down to say hello. I was content to just watch their actions and wasn't sure I wanted anything more to do with them. I had no intention of having the grapevine say that I had been a party to investigating my fellow trainers. I had a lot of friends among these guys and would not betray those friendships.

It worked out well for me that they left while my last horse was on the track. I didn't have to run into them when I came out of the grandstand on my way to the barn. The rest of the day I was busy running my horses, and they kind of faded out of mind.

The next morning I had two fillies and a colt scheduled to work. The fillies were of different caliber, one being an older, mature campaigner, and the other an unraced maiden. I didn't plan to work them together. The colt worked first and I had entered the time in my notebook when I noticed the guys down on the apron watching the horses. I hadn't seen them come out and didn't have any idea how long they had been there.

Goodman had exchanged his slacks for jeans and both wore polo shirts again. I watched as I waited for my next horse, which was just galloping today. They again struck up no serious conversation and just moved among the people on the apron in an aimless manner. When the older filly came on the track and her name was announced to work, they must have recognized her as one of my horses, because they began to look around for me. I was relieved when they spotted me and just waved rather than come up to talk. I returned the wave but did not give them any sign that I wanted them to join me.

The next few days were typical of life on the track. The day-to-day sameness of caring for horses can appear to be boring but isn't, because every time you handle a horse, you are just a heartbeat away from a catastrophe. It can be caused by a mistake or a mental lapse or through no fault of anyone. A horse can hurt himself or you in the blink of an eye, with no apparent cause. Racing is especially dangerous because the horses are wound as tight as possible and kept in a confined stall without enough opportunity to release their pent-up energy. It is never boring although it is repetitive.

The guys were at the track every morning during training but did not approach me, although they waved every day. I had to assume they had given up on bringing me into whatever they had planned. I was relived to be clear of any racetrack investigation, but I was curious about what they were doing here. I had not mentioned them to anyone because I didn't think I should raise any red flags when I had no clue what it was all about.

Monday was a dark day with no racing scheduled. The morning was pretty laid back since there no rush to get things done by a certain time, and most of the crew had the afternoon off. We were finished and I was sitting in the office doing the last of my paperwork when my cell phone rang.

"Mr. Holden, this is Robert Goodman. I would like to speak with you this afternoon if you have some free time."

I had intended to drive over to Pomona to look at a two year old a friend had called me about. He was about ready to go to the races and was for sale. My friend had been training him and his owner was involved in a divorce; he had to sell all three of his horses by court order. That would only take about an hour so I said, "What time did you want to meet?"

He said, "I am free all afternoon. You tell me when and I will meet you wherever you like."

"I am going to Pomona to look at a horse that's for sale, but it shouldn't take more than an hour or so. I could meet you after that."

He paused before asking, "Is it something I might be interested in?"

"I doubt it. He is an unraced two-year old and that's not usually where a first-time owner should invest. You could hit a home run, but more often you lose most of you investment."

"Would you mind if I rode along? Afterwards we could stop for a bite to eat and have a talk."

"Where are you?"

"I'm sitting in my car in the horsemen's parking lot."

That caused me to blink a couple of times before I answered, "I'll be out in about ten minutes. Watch for me at the stable gate."

As I walked through the stable area on my way to the parking lot, I was posing questions in my mind that I needed answers for. He was going to answer them to my satisfaction or our association would be over before it ever started. I had no intention of being a shill for these guys without knowing what I was involved in. He would need a very compelling reason to rope me into his game. I had a business that took unending attention to details, and I didn't need distractions; nor was I about to let them make enemies for me among the other horsemen.

He was standing at the gate when I came out and greeted me friendly enough although he had to realize I had not been pursuing any contact with them in the week they had been coming to the track every morning. I drove my pickup because I wanted to be in my own vehicle in case we weren't friends after we had our conversation. I didn't want to be left stranded in a parking lot somewhere watching him drive away.

The drive to Pomona only takes fifteen or twenty minutes at that time of day, and neither one of us had much to say. I didn't want to ask questions until there was enough time for a complete answer. Pomona is a training center except during a short race meet that is held every year in conjunction with the county fair. When it is a training center, the security is much more lax than at a race meet; I just waved at the guard as we walked through the gate. I stable babies here from time to time and am here a lot, so they all know me.

We went to my friend's barn and found him on the phone ordering feed. I listened with amusement while he complained about the last load of bedding straw they had brought him. He wasn't happy with the quality and wasn't getting any sympathy from the person on the other end of the line. His voice was slowing getting louder until he noticed me smiling. That made him aware he was getting agitated over something that couldn't be changed; he smiled at me and broke off the conversation.

I introduced Goodman and we went out to see the horse. I liked him immediately when he led him out of the stall. He had nice size and conformation. Another one of the things you learn early in this business is you can wear the tires off your pickup driving around to look at horses that people call you about. I will only go if it is someone that I know very well. This trainer and I had been friends for a long time and I knew him to be a good horseman. We had stabled in the same barn together several times and I trusted his judgment of a horse. I wouldn't have come otherwise, but I was pleasantly surprised at the quality of this colt.

As I walked around the colt checking for faults, the trainer was giving me an account of where the colt was in his training program. He was at the point that most trainers would be looking for a race for him, but my friend was thinking about another thirty days. I would certainly take the advice of the person who had been working with the colt since day one and give him the thirty days if I bought him. I examined him from every angle and liked everything I saw. The only thing that might keep me from buying him was the price. He had said on the phone he was worth the money but had not named the price. I normally would not buy a horse without seeing him under tack but knowing the caliber of horseman I was dealing with I decided that would just be wasting time for both of us.

We went back to the office and he offered us sodas. We sat down and made ourselves comfortable before I asked the big question. "How much?"

"You are in luck because the court ordered the owner to sell him within thirty days, and that has kind of panicked him. He bought this colt for forty thousand in the yearling sale at Keenland. He seems to think it's like buying a new car in that you lose money as soon as you drive it off the show room floor. He wants twenty-five thousand and might take less if you offered."

I didn't hesitate with my answer. "I don't see any point in trying to squeeze the guy for a few dollars when I consider the twenty-five to be a fair price. I'll have him. You want a check now?"

"The papers are already in the office at Santa Anita. Since you'll need a bill of sale from him for the stewards to transfer them into your name, why don't I have him come to the track in the morning and you just give him the check when he makes out the bill of sale?"

I stood up and extended my hand in a good-bye gesture and said, "That will work for me. I appreciate the call, and if I can ever help you out don't hesitate."

As we walked back to the parking lot, Goodman asked, "Did you buy this horse for yourself?"

"I have to offer him to my clients first. If none of them want another horse, I will race him for myself."

"When you say you have to offer him to your clients first, is that a rule of racing?"

"No, that's a rule of getting along with your clients. The racing game is a funny business and everyone is suspicious as hell. If he turned out to be a good one and I hadn't offered him to my clients, someone would be sure to say, 'Sure, you offer us the questionable ones and keep the good ones for yourself.'"

"Do you race many horses of your own?"

"I like to keep two or three running. It gives me options on stalls. The racetrack is always short of stalls, and if all of your stalls are full and one of your clients wants to claim a horse you have no place to put him. If I have two or three of my own, I can always take one of them over to Pomona to make room for the new horse. I couldn't send any owner's horses over there without making them mad. If you have an empty stall for very long, the track will take it away from you. Moving one of my horses out doesn't happen a lot because the horses of clients are claimed at about the same rate as they are claiming them."

"Do you have a lot of horses claimed from you?"

"Not as many as I should. This is another quirk of this business. As soon as a horse wins a race, the owner insists that you raise him in claiming price so he will not be claimed. This is fine except that they keep raising them until they are at a level where they can't win. Now you are stuck with a horse that can't win but can't be lowered in claiming price because the owner can't bear to lose him. It's a Catch-22, and I have never devised a way to overcome it. Half of the horses in my barn are running over their head."

"Do the horses you own get claimed often?"

"Fairly often. In the course of a year, I'll have eight or ten claimed from me, and I'll claim about the same number. Since I only own two or three, that's a high rate of claiming activity. If no one is interested and I keep this horse for myself, I'll need to get one of mine claimed to make room for him."

"How do you go about getting one claimed?"

"That's a simple process. Let's say that I have a horse that is a solid thirty thousand dollar horse. By solid I mean he always lights the board and wins a decent percentage of races at thirty. If I drop him in at twenty, I will get my money back because the winner's share is more than ten thousand and he is an odds-on favorite to win. If the drop scares them off because they are afraid there is something wrong with him, I will run him down their throat and win every twenty thousand dollar race until they are forced to take him. I like that scenario because it lets me make money in the meanwhile."

I pulled into Bob's Big Boy without asking if it suited him. I just wanted a place to get a sandwich and do some straight talking. I waited until the waitress had taken our order and walked away before I said, "Okay, tell me what this is all about. Are you FBI?"

"Yes, both St. Germaine and I are members of the FBI. I knew that you didn't believe we really wanted to be racehorse owners, but the truth is we are actually going to buy a horse. We got the okay Friday and they gave us fifty thousand dollars to work with. We are not asking anything from you except the training of our horse."

"That's not the explanation I need from you. I am not going to allow my name to be associated with an investigation of my fellow trainers. It's a tough enough business without having everyone connected with it thinking I am untrustworthy."

"I understand that, but I assure you we are not investigating horseracing in any way."

"Then why do you need to be at the racetrack?"

"St. Germaine and I are members of a task force established to find a professional assassin. This man has been operating for at least ten years and has a long string of kills behind him. It was several years before we even realized it was just one person. He is very good and can kill in numerous ways. The assassinations have taken place all over the country. The only thing that they have in common is that all of the victims are wealthy business people. This is perplexing because we can't establish connections between any of them other than wealth. There doesn't appear to be any gambling or drugs or anything illegal about any of their activities."

"How do you know it's a man and not some deranged high class hooker?"

"We're fairly certain it's a man because several of the kills have been by hand: a couple of broken necks, a crushed larynx, two were garroted—one with such force it nearly took his head off—and three were killed with an ice pick or something similar, placed expertly in the heart. The only regular occurrence has been by shooting. The weapon of chose is a silenced twenty-two. This is what first alerted us that these kills might all be done by the same person."

"Have any of the victims been connected to racing?"

"A few have, but only in the sense they are wealthy and can afford to own racehorses. None in any capacity other than as owners."

"You still haven't explained why you should be at the race track."

"I have to admit the reason we want to be here is very thin. This guy is driving us crazy, and we will clutch at any straw that floats by. About six months ago, a very wealthy businessman, who fits the profile of the victims, was found shot to death in the men's room at LAX. He had just flown in from Hawaii and was traveling with a couple of friends. They had gone down to pick up the luggage and he had made a quick stop, which indicates that the assassin was waiting for a chance at him. The thing that gets interesting here is that later that day a cab was found a few blocks away from the airport with the driver and two passengers shot dead by the same gun, a silenced twenty-two."

"You are telling me that a guy who is so perfect that you didn't know he existed for several years suddenly goes drugstore cowboy and shoots someone in the men's room of a crowded airport like LAX? He then gets in a cab with two passengers and kills everyone in the cab? That doesn't make a lot of sense."

"I know it doesn't, and we are trying to find out what was special about this guy that made him a rush job. This is the first time our man has ever not had it planned to the last detail."

"You still haven't explained what connects him to the racetrack."

"It turned out that the driver worked the airport as a regular, but the two passengers had just flown in from San Francisco where they had gone to take care of a horse sent up for a stakes race. Their plane arrived about the same time as the plane from Hawaii. Now we are just guessing, but we think that the two grooms were in the airport during the shooting and saw our shooter, although they didn't know about the shooting. The important thing is they knew the shooter and could place him there. We think he offered to let them share his cab to the track, which at that time was Hollywood Park. They would have jumped at the chance to save cab fare, not knowing anything about the as yet undiscovered shooting. The cab driver was just unlucky collateral damage. We ran a thorough background of everyone that had any connection to the stable the grooms worked for but didn't find a suspect among them. It must have been a chance meeting of someone they knew from the track. Nothing else makes sense."

"I remember when the two grooms were shot. The rumor was one of them had cashed a big bet in San Francisco and they were robbed for it. I didn't personally know either one of them, but it was talked about for several days."

"We don't expect to see our man doing the deed and catch him red-handed. All we are trying to do is get some idea of the life style and routine of racetrack people. We need to have some knowledge of how racetrack people move around, and why they move around, so we can began to check out people that made moves that weren't consistent with what would have been normal. Of course anyone that is on the weird side would be of interest to us."

"If you are going to check out everyone on the racetrack that seems weird, you will look like a dog chasing his tale. Half of them are certifiably crazy and are only here because they can't survive in the outside world. They need this guarded environment to keep them safe from the normal world."

"Maybe you could give me a couple examples of what you mean by weird."

"I have a little farm out north of Los Angeles, and a few years ago they put in a training track near me. Every few weeks I would stop by when I was in the area to see what was going on. At a training track, people come and go quite often, and it had new faces most every time I stopped.

"One morning I stopped by, and a trainer who had won a breeders cup—which puts him in the big time—had moved in with a few horses. I walked up to the track and found him laid out on a towel next to the track in a pair of Speedos sunbathing while he watched his horses train. I thought that a little weird. Although I didn't know what he was doing at the time, I'm ninety percent sure I saw him slip the Speedos on when he saw me approaching.

"A few years ago, I bought a mare from a trainer with a big and successful stable. He eventually moved to Kentucky to be a private trainer for one of the biggest farms in the country. He told me that the papers were at home, and I could pick them up the first time I was up that way. I had bought her as a broodmare prospect so I didn't mind waiting for the papers. One Monday afternoon I was in his area and called to ask if I could pick up the papers. He told me he was at the pool and to come on around back. I opened the gate and went around. He was lying on a chase lounge in his swim trunks with a pitcher of sangria on the table beside him. He was on the high side of two hundred and seventy pounds and looked like a beached whale. He was watching the action in the pool, which contained eight or ten girls wearing only fingernail polish.

"He said to me, 'Sit down and enjoy the show. That's all you can do because they are all lesbians.' Then he roared with laughter.

"I knew he had a lot of girls working for him, but I had never given it much thought. I thought that was a little weird, but I must admit, I did sit for awhile.

"In the middle of the afternoon, I was going around the corner of a barn when I came upon an old trainer. He was sitting in front of a stall in an overstuffed living room chair. He had been a very successful trainer in his prime but was now in his eighties.

"I said to him, What in the world are you doing?

"Without even looking my way, he said, 'this son of a bitch is not running well and I am going to sit right here until he tells me what's wrong.'

"Those sorts of things go on all the time it's not even strange to me anymore. I could go on relating stories of that type for hours, but no one among them is a murderer."

"It sounds like abnormal behavior is normal here, but that isn't what our man is going to be. He is a cool and calculating type and will try to stay out of the spotlight. Killing the two grooms tells us that he will eliminate any threat, real or imagined, without hesitation. For that reason I would suggest that you never mention this to anyone, not even your closest friend. I know a man never thinks his close friend could be a killer, but believe me when I tell you this is going to be someone you would never suspect. He couldn't have gotten away with it for over ten years otherwise. Have you ever seen any of these guy exhibit unexpected violent behavior?" Goodman asked.

"I have seen violent behavior a time or two, but it wasn't altogether unexpected."

"What do you mean wasn't unexpected?"

"Either the situation forced the person into a violent reaction or it was normal behavior that I had already been warned of or heard stories about."

"Give me an example."

"There is a trainer named John Borden, who is a legend around the racetrack for his fighting ability. One afternoon I was sitting in a bar having a drink with some friends and John was at a table nearby with his friends. I was sitting with my back against the wall looking towards the bar. The door opened and a weight lifter type walked in. He had arms the size of my thighs and a short sleeve shirt with the sleeves so tight they may have been cutting off his circulation. He stopped at the bar and talked to the bartender for a second, and then the bartender pointed back toward John. John was sitting with his back to the bar and didn't see this. The guy came back to John's table and because John had his back to him had to move into the gap between the two tables in order to be sort of facing John.

"When he said, 'Are you John Borden?' John slid his chair back from the table and answered with a curt 'Yes.' The guy then said, 'Mr. Greenstein asked me to come by and talk to you on his behalf. Let's go out to the parking lot.'

"As he was saying this, John stood up. He now said, 'I don't think so. You might change your mind by the time we get there.' and hit him. He hit the guy so hard his head knocked a hole in the drywall behind him. He went down on his face and lay there with his legs jerking in some kind of spasm. I thought he had killed him. I've never seen anyone hit that hard in my life. I've seen men kicked by horses many times and it didn't make the sound him hitting that guy made. It took two of John's friends fifteen or twenty minutes to get the man revived enough for them to help him out to his car. John meanwhile calmly sat there and drank his beer. I call that violent behavior, but because of the stories I had heard it wasn't unexpected."

"That's not the kind of man I'm looking for. Can you give me other examples?"

"Some years back there was a trainer I had been warned to stay away from. I didn't need much warning because he was huge. Everyone called him by the nickname of Hunk. One afternoon Greg Schwartz claimed a horse from him. After the race Greg was walking down the road to his barn and Hunk ran over him with his pickup. It hurt Greg pretty bad. It broke one of his arms and four ribs and he was so bruised and scraped up that it was hard to recognize him. When I asked Greg what he was going to do about it, he said, 'Are you crazy? Look what he did to me just for claiming a horse from him. What do you think he would do if I had him put in jail?'"

"These guys are habitually violent. Our man is going to be someone who would surprise the hell out of you when he shows that side of himself."

In the meantime the waitress had brought our food and we ate in silence while I thought it over. I decided that it shouldn't cause me any problems and I gave him my answer. "I will try to find you a horse; but I promise you that if the horsemen become even the slightest bit suspicious, I will cut you lose. I can't afford to have a bad reputation among the people I do business with."

"That is good enough for me. How about my taking the horse you just bought? You seemed to like him."

"I don't have a problem with that as long as you understand that an unraced horse is a gamble. He may not be worth anything."

"I fully understand and will not complain if that turns out to be the case. I am in a unique situation because the money they have approved for this project is already written off as an expense. I am just looking for a reason to be around and hoping to get enough of an education about racing to spot something out of line."

He paid the bill and I left a tip for the waitress. We drove back to the track without much conversation. I dropped him at his car and went on home. I had several phone calls to make to owners. I tried to make contact with every owner at least once a week to discuss his horses and races that might be coming up. It is one of the unpleasant aspects of the business, but it is necessary to keep everyone happy.

I remember one of the few times that I ever felt true envy of another trainer. I was sitting in the kitchen at Hollywood Park with a friend having lunch. A couple of tables away Bobby Frankel was at a table going over some paperwork with one of his assistants. Two well-dressed older gentlemen came in and walked over to Bobby's table. One of them, who obviously knew Bobby, introduced the other one and said the man was looking for a trainer.

Bobby stood up shook the newcomer's hand and said, "Let me tell you how I work. I send you a bill and you send me a check. I call you when your horse is in a race and you come to the races to watch him run. Other than that, I don't want to see you, and I don't want to hear from you. If you can live with that, we will sit down and talk about your horse."

I remember thinking, Wow! Bobby is my hero for life. I would give my first born to have the nerve to tell clients that. Of course I wouldn't have any business, but I would starve to death a very contented man.

I spent the entire afternoon on the phone and was exhausted from the effort. It is hard to keep owners happy because they always think their horses are better than they actually are. People tend to live in a fantasy world, thinking they are just a race away from fame and fortune when in reality their horses should be running a few notches below where they are running. You have to walk a fine line between massaging their ego and insulting them by telling them they're nuts. It's one of the hardest parts of the business.

The next morning I was at my spot in the grandstand when Goodman and his sidekick came in. As soon as they saw me, they came up to where I was sitting. After saying their hellos, Goodman got down to business. "I brought a cashier's check for twenty-five thousand. Have we heard from the owner yet?"

"Not yet, but I'm sure we will. If I haven't heard from him by the end of training, I'll call my friend. You guys go ahead and do your thing and I'll look you up as soon as I hear from him."

Between watching my horses train, I kept an eye on them. They were just hanging out. Watching the horses on the track and having casual conversations with various people. Most of the people that were available for chitchat were casual gamblers, watching the horses train and hoping to pick up something that would give them an edge. They weren't going to learn much about racetrack life talking to them, but I wasn't going to start offering unasked for advice. I intended to stay as divorced from their activities as possible.

It was a few minutes after nine and my last horse was just leaving the track when my cell phone rang. It was my friend from Pomona calling to tell me that the owner would meet me in the stewards' office at eleven o'clock, if that was good for me. It was, and as I came down from the grandstand, I stopped to tell the boys. They were at a loss for a way to kill the next two hours so I took them back to the barn with me.

When we reached the barn, I found a jockey agent hanging around waiting to talk to me. It was obvious that he didn't know me very well. The agents for all of the jockeys that I normally ride know where to find me in the grandstand during training hours. I usually have three or four stop by every morning to ask if I have any business for them.

He wanted to tell me about a new jock that he had brought to town from El Paso. The jock had been third leading rider at Sunland Park and wanted to take a shot at the big time. A new jockey is a tough sell for an agent unless he came with a stable who can give him mounts. A normal trainer is not going to ride a rider without having seen him in action. An agent has the problem of getting mounts for people to watch him ride when trainers won't ride him until they have seen him ride. It was another Catch-22. I explained my position and thanked him for coming by. One thing that a good agent must do is accept rejection well. Unless they have a really top rider, they spend most of their time hearing rejection. They may ask for a hundred mounts a day to end up on two or three—if they are lucky. I have always wondered how jocks and their agents make it when they are at the bottom of the ladder. Some of these guys only ride two or three horses a week.

Before I called to inform the stewards that we would be there at eleven, I asked how they were going to take title. Was it going to be a partnership or just one of them listed as sole owner? They hadn't thought about it and after discussing it decided they had to make it a partnership in order for both of them to be licensed. I called and made the appointment and we had nothing to do but wait.

I started doing my paperwork, and they wandered out into the shed row to watch the stable routine. At this time of day there wasn't much to see. Most of the work was over, and the grooms were just cleaning up and preparing to close up the barn for the day. They wouldn't have anything else to do today except feed and water this evening and touch up the bedding. If I was running a horse this afternoon, the groom who handled that particular horse would have to stay until after the race to help me run him and to take care of him afterwards; otherwise they had the afternoon off.

A few minutes before eleven we walked over to the stewards' office. At most of the smaller tracks, when you went to the office, if the door was open you walked in. If the door was closed, it meant they were conducting business and you waited until they opened it. Here they had an outer office with a secretary, and she notified them you were waiting. The owner was already waiting and got up to introduce himself, and I explained that two of my clients were taking ownership of the horse. We waited about fifteen minutes before the secretary informed us we could go in.

I explained to the stewards that they were new owners and would apply for their license as soon as we had completed the transfer of ownership. There wasn't anything unusual about this and we were finished in ten minutes. I walked them down to the racing board office for their license and left them to do the paperwork.

Fortunately I had an empty stall and called the company that did most of my hauling to have the horse picked up. They were experienced enough to know they had to contact the current trainer to arrange a time for the pickup. They promised to make it tomorrow, if possible. I have a four-horse trailer and haul my own horses, but I make it a point to never haul a client's horse. The liability is too high.

The next morning was business as usual. I knew that the horse wouldn't be delivered until after the track closed for training because they wouldn't allow the van into the stable area until then. I went to my spot in the grandstand as soon as we sent our first horse to the track. I wasn't surprised to see that Goodman was already there waiting for me. I could understand that he was excited about the new horse, but I hoped he didn't intend to spend mornings with me in the grandstand. I used that time for my horses and didn't appreciate distractions. I was relieved when I told him that the horse wouldn't be delivered until after training hours and he went on down to the apron.

When my last horse came off the track, I walked back to the barn and found Goodman and St. Germaine both waiting at the barn. They were as excited as any new owner would be in the same situation. The thought crossed my mind that they might prove to be a pain in the butt. It is bad enough to have to deal with real owners, and I would surely begrudge having to spend a lot of extra time educating fake owners.

The van company called to tell me the horse would arrive about one o'clock. I gave the groom that would be handling him the information and we walked over to the kitchen for a bite to eat. We went through the line and got our food before we even decided where to sit. Judging from the piled tray of Goodman, I was pretty sure he had skipped breakfast to get here early.

We ate in silence, and when we were finished, Goodman opened with an observation. "I think we are wasting our time at the grandstand in the mornings. The people that we are meeting don't know anything about horsemen. They only talk about bets they have won and lost and horses they like and dislike."

I smiled as I said, "It didn't take long for you to pick up on that. With the exception of a few old timers that come out every now and then just to feel a little nostalgic, not many of those people have ever been on the backside. You need to hang out right here where the horsemen hang out. You'll hear more racetrack news and gossip in two or three hours sitting in one of those card games than you'll hear in a month at the grandstand in the mornings. Talking to a gambler about horseracing is like talking to a cheer leader about basketball. You'll get a lot of enthusiasm but not much knowledge about how to play the game."

He didn't think my wit was all that amusing and said, "You could have warned me that we were going about it wrong."

"No, I don't think so. You need to be exposed to all the players to fully understand the business. Besides, you don't know that your man is not among the gamblers. It is not unthinkable that one of the regular gamblers would be known by one of those grooms. Some of the bigger gamblers often offer grooms a hundred or two for information on the horses."

Goodman's face went slack as he said, "Oh my god. I had never considered that, and if that is the case we may never catch this guy except by accident."

"It's something you need to consider. It's not very likely, but you can't ignore the fact that it's a possibility. We should be getting back; the van could be arriving any time now."

As we walked back to the barn, I could tell I had spoiled his day. The van was pulling up as we came around the barn. It was perfect timing and we watched as the horse was unloaded. I ran my hands over the legs after the groom had removed the shipping wraps and felt no heat or swelling. I had the groom put him in his stall and feed and water him. I wouldn't bother him anymore today. He needed time to relax and get accustomed to his new surroundings.

The next morning I checked him again. I would have given him a day or two to adjust, but I was afraid that he hadn't been out of his stall since I had agreed to buy him. I had him tacked up and put my best exercise rider aboard.

I only have two exercise riders on my payroll and use freelance riders for part of my work. Because freelance riders are not very reliable, you can't count on them showing up every day. We can get all of the horses out with two riders if we have to, but it makes a tough day for everyone. My best rider is a girl that I hired from the polo grounds at Griffith Park. I have hired two or three girls from there and they make exceptional exercise riders. They exercise the polo ponies four at a time. They ride one while leading two on the right side and one on the left side. Most of them were good riders before they started with the polo horses, but after a year or two of that kind of work they are excellent. They think they are on easy street when they come to the track and only gallop one horse at a time.

I had the groom lead the horse to the track to insure that he didn't get in a wreck because of the strange surroundings. I went to the grandstand to watch and was pleased with the way he went. He looked at a few things but didn't get overly excited and had a nice way of going. He was going to fit right in.

The guys had come to the barn early and waited around to watch him train. They followed him to the track and followed him back to the barn. They both acted as if they had just had a baby, and I expected them to start handing out cigars at any minute.

I waited until they had tired of hanging around the barn and gone to the kitchen before I questioned the rider. She gave him a good report in all aspects and liked him. She had been with me long enough to know that I didn't want anything sugar-coated, so if she said he was good I'm sure he was. One less thing to worry about and I could get back to normal training.

The week went in a steady, routine way. The boys were out every morning to watch their horse and spent the afternoons in the kitchen playing cards and getting acquainted with racetrack people. I ran five horses and won two races, making it a normal week. I sent the new horse to break from the starting gate on Friday.

I wasn't expecting any problem with him from the gate. Training at Pomona has an advantage for young horses. The entrance to the track is at the end of the chute and a four horse gate sits in the chute with front and rear doors all open. A lot of the trainers have the riders walk them through the gate every morning when they come on the track. Sometimes they walk straight through, and sometimes they stop and stand in the gate for a while before they go on. It's good training for a young horse, and I have never had gate problems with a horse broke and trained there. This horse was no exception; he walked right in, stood quietly, and broke very well.

Monday morning I worked him for my first time. I worked him five-eighths of a mile, and he went in a very respectable time of a minute and two-fifths. He came back not even blowing, and I realized he was fitter than I thought. The boys had come to watch the work and asked a million questions. I answered some of them and just shrugged my shoulders to some. I told them the horse would walk for the next two days and they didn't need to come out.

As they were getting ready to leave, Goodman came into the office and said, "Don't leave until I get back from the car. I have something I want you to look over."

I was nearly finished and told him, "Then come right back. I am taking a date sailing this afternoon and I need to go pretty quick."

He wasn't gone more than ten minutes. He laid a two inch thick stack of paper on my desk and said, "I would appreciate you looking through this when you get a chance. I need to know if anything jumps out at you."

"What is it?"

"It is a computer printout of everyone who is licensed to be on the racetrack in California that has also served in the military."

"Why the military?"

"Our forensics people tell us that some of the kills were made by methods taught in the military."

"I'll look through it when I get time, but that is a lot of names. Since you have all of this computer power, why don't you run a list of all the people licensed in every state where you think he made a kill? That should be a much shorter list, and if you think he's using the track as a hiding place, he has to be licensed in each state."

"That's exactly the reason we're here. We aren't going to think of those things because we don't know how it works. I assumed that it was like a driver's license and was honored in every state."

"I'm glad to be of some help, but I have to go now or I'm going to be late. I'll see you in the morning."

Since his horse wasn't training for a couple of days, I didn't expect to see him the next morning; but when I came back to the barn from the track, he was waiting for me. He handed me a much shorter list. This one was only about ten pages, but it was still a lot of names.

"Take a look at this list first. I would like for you to still look through the big list, but give this one a once-over first."

"I'll look at it this afternoon. Is it everyone who is cross licensed or just the ones that were in the military?"

"It's just the military people. We have to start somewhere and the fewer people to check out the better. If nothing promising turns up, we'll expand our list later."

"You don't really expect me to find a killer by looking through this list of names."

"No, but sometimes looking through a list of the people you know will trigger memories of things that happened in the past you had completely forgotten. You might remember something that was said about one of them that at the time had no significance but now might mean more to you."

"What kind of things?"

"What if you overheard two guys talking and one of them was telling the other what happened in the bar last night. He says you should have seen Joe put the guy down. It was so quick the guy didn't know what hit him. When you heard it, you had no reason to give it a second thought; but now you know we are looking for a guy who can do that sort of thing. All I ask is that look through the names in case you think of something."

"I'll look, but it sounds far-fetched to me."

"It is, but like I said, we are clutching at straws here."

As we were talking, I was scanning the printout he had handed me, and I could see that he didn't understand what he needed to do. "Let me explain how this works. You will need to print out the people that were licensed during the timeframe that the murders were committed in each state. In most states a license is for one year only, and if the crime was two years ago, he may not be licensed this year. In fact you may get a good lead by only printing the people that were licensed in every state where the murders occurred during the year in which they took place. No one is going to be licensed in every state every year unless he is a mega-trainer or owner with hundreds of horses. That kind of person is not going to have time to wait in an airport on the chance he might get a shot at an arriving passenger.

"You might also check with security to see if van drivers must be licensed to deliver a horse to the track. A van driver for a big outfit might go to tracks all over the country, and I can't believe they would go through the licensing process to drop off one horse and maybe never come to that track again."

He looked a little long faced as he said, "This could turn out to be an impossible task, couldn't it?"

"It might not be impossible, but it will certainly be difficult. You have to remember that a racetrack only runs for two or three months and then the horsemen all move on to a new track. They don't all move to the same track. They scatter all over the country. I may see a trainer here every year and not see him again until the meet opens here next year. In some cases I may not see a certain trainer but once every three or four years. It all depends on where his home base is and where most of his owners are. It is a very nomadic way of life. A trainer has to go where his owners want to run, and he has to go where his horses fit. If you don't have horses that are competitive at Santa Anita, you can't afford to come here knowing you aren't going to win any races."

"Obviously the first thing to do is see how many people show up in the states where the hits took place during the correct times. I would think that list is going to be smaller. I'll get back to you when we get a new printout."

After he left I sat looking through the printout he had given me. The thing that was most surprising about the list was the number of horsemen that had been in the military. Horsemen are notoriously loose cannons. If you put a dozen horsemen in the same room, you can't get an agreement on anything—I doubt you could get them to agree on what day of the week it was. It was hard to believe that this many of them had been exposed to military discipline without landing in jail for insubordination.

The following week was busy for me. I had at least one horse in every afternoon and took most of my horses to the track every morning. After training every morning, I spent an hour or two in the racing office entering horses, and waiting for the draw to see if I got in a race, and what post position I drew. I didn't get a lot of chances to talk to the boys even though they came every day. They would hang around the barn until their horse went to the track and then spend the rest of the day in the kitchen. I guess Goodman taught St. Germaine to play racehorse because the couple of times I stopped in they were both in games at different tables.

Most of the trainers don't go to the draw because they let the jockey agent for whichever riders they are using handle anything that comes up. I have been jerked around a couple of times doing that and always go to the draw. Agents don't always honor their commitment to ride your horse, and if you aren't at the draw you may get a rider you don't like. Because most all of the agents are there every day, you get to know them pretty well. They come across as good friends, but you must keep reminding yourself they want to do business with you. If you didn't have horses they want to ride, they might not give you the time of day. They are agents, after all, which is another name for salesmen.

I had to go to Phoenix on Saturday to saddle a horse I had shipped over for a low-end stakes race. I had hoped for a win but had to settle for second. The owner wasn't happy, and I was tired on the flight back. It took a great effort on my part to not say something I would regret later. I had to explain several times that the horse was sound and fit and had just been outrun. There were no excuses. He simply was not the best horse in the race. He didn't get a bad ride; he didn't get in trouble during the race; he just got outrun. I put up with all of the whining I could stand before I finally said, "Mr. Doyle, did you look at the time of the race? Even though he ran second, your horse just ran the fastest race of his life. Unfortunately there was a faster horse in the race and that is horseracing. I opened my note pad and started making entries to let him know the conversation was over.

When I arrived home, the news was a little better. My assistant had saddled a horse I had in here and he had won. That didn't take the sting completely away, but it helped. A friend of mine's favorite saying is that trainers are used to losing because their horses lose eighty percent of the time. Horseracing has a lot of ups and downs and the ups never seem to override the disappointments of the downs.

You never know how a race is going to end until it's over. I remember one day I was in the racing office, and they were having trouble filling races. I had entered a horse in a race that he was a mortal lock to win, but the race only had six horses and was probably not going to be used. The racing secretary called me in and asked me to enter a filly in another race that I didn't like for her. I told him I would enter her in that race if he would use the other race with only six horses. He was desperate enough to finally agree. The sacrifice filly ran in an early race and won by two lengths while the mortal lock I loved in his spot ran a bad third, beaten six lengths. If you ever start thinking you have this business figured out, it means you are a candidate for the loony bin.

Sunday was a drab, overcast day with a forecast for a sixty percent chance of rain. In Southern California it can go for months without a drop of rain, but during the rainy season it may rain for three weeks without a break. I had two horses in and hoped the rain held off until the races were over. Both of the horses could run on an off track, but I wasn't in the mood to get wet and muddy. I was tired and in a bad mood, and the second and fourth my horses ran didn't do anything to lighten it. I was glad the next two days were dark and planned to relax both afternoons.

Monday I worked Goodman's horse a half mile out of the gate, and he went perfect. I didn't know if there was already a gate card in the office and asked the starter for a gate OK, just in case one wasn't on file. The boys were there to watch, of course, and although they didn't really understand the importance of a young horse working well from the gate, they liked what they saw.

After training, Goodman brought me two printouts. One was only about four pages and included everyone who had undergone military training and was licensed in the right state at the right time. The other was a listing of everyone in the right state at the right time. This list was about twenty pages.

Goodman said, "We are running a background check on everyone that made the first list. I should have that in a couple of days, but I can't show it to you. It might contain confidential material and I could get in trouble for sharing it with a civilian."

"That's fine with me. I have no interest in who beat his wife or didn't pay his credit card bill. I am going to spend this afternoon on my boat and will try to give these lists my attention. I'm not taking the boat out. I'm just going down to hang out and get a little R & R."

I have a thirty-two foot Coronado sloop that I keep at Marina Del Rey. I love the old wood boats, and some of them have gorgeous lines; but when you are in a seven-days-a-week business, you don't have time for the maintenance and upkeep required for them. My boat is fiberglass and gets a hose turned on it once a week or so. That's about all of the time I can spare for maintenance.

I don't get to sail as much as I would like, but it makes a great hideaway on those afternoons when I feel a need for solitude. This was such an afternoon. It was comfortable and private and many times I spent the night and went to the track straight from the boat. It was large enough to have all of the comforts of home and yet small enough I can sail solo when the urge strikes me. I have roller furling on my sails and single handling is not a problem. My only complaint is I wish the shower was a little more spacious.

I stopped for a bite to eat on the way and didn't get there until after two. I spent a couple of hours hosing off the outside and cleaning the cabin. I took my laundry up to the dockside laundry room and put everything in order before settling down to look at the printouts.

I started with the small printout and went through it quickly, putting a check mark beside every name that I recognized. Then I went name by name, trying to conjure up a picture of each name and going over everything that I could remember about that person. It was slow work because most of the time, recalling one person would cause me to recall other people and stories that I remembered or had heard. I had to keep bringing myself back to the person in question. By the time I reached the end of the four page list, I think I had relived most of my racing life. I was exhausted and surprised to see that it was eight o'clock.

I was starving and decided to drive somewhere to get something to eat. I had food on board and a full galley, but I didn't feel like cooking. Several steak houses are available in the marina, but they are all in conjunction with a nightclub, and I wasn't in the mood for that. I drove out of the marina and a few blocks up the coast highway to a little restaurant where I had eaten before. I was thankful I didn't run into anyone I knew and ate in peace still thinking about all of the memories I had dredged up looking through the list.

I had not found anyone that I even remotely thought of as a killer, but I had seen a few names that reminded me of people I hadn't seen in a long time. Some I didn't like much, but there had been a couple of names of people I liked, and I hoped were doing well. One in particular stood out.

He had stabled near me for a couple of years and we had become good friends. He had been in the racing game most of his life, starting as a quarter horse rider as a kid and becoming a trainer when he grew too large to be a rider. He had ended up training for a superstar country singer. The singer had fallen out of favor and went several years without a hit. He had finally disbanded his racing stable and my friend had spent the next few years with a small public stable and kind of struggling. After several years the singer had out of the blue come up with a mega-hit that was one of the top songs of the decade. He followed that up with another really good hit and was back in the chips. He rehired my friend as a farm manager for a farm he owned in Texas, and I had not seen him since.

But some of the stories he had related about his life were fantastic. When he was riding quarter horses, he had traveled the country with an owner/trainer racing at fairs, little tracks, and anywhere they could find a race. They had stopped in a small town to run at a fair and had a decent horse. The night before the race a gentleman had come to their hotel and introduced himself as the owner of one the horses they were going to race against. He offered the trainer three hundred dollars to not outrun his horse. It was a matter of pride to him to be the big man in the area. Since that was about what the winner would receive, the trainer agreed and took the money. When they were getting ready for the race, the trainer pulled their horse trailer up beside the barn and packed all of their gear. He told the rider to win the race, come straight to the barn, and put the horse on the trailer because they were leaving town as soon as possible. This was an indication of what low-end racing was like in those days. No testing of the winners or anything else: Run your horse in a race, put him on the trailer, and go.

Another story he told me was that he was riding at a fair meet in the Midwest. As a promotion the fair had paid Eddie Arcaro to come and ride in a race. My friend was on a horse that had no chance to even hit the board so he decided that he would make the best showing he could for the owner by blasting away from the gate and trying to put the horse on the lead for as long as he could hold on. As they turned down the stretch, Eddie came gliding by, and my friend reached down and grabbed a handful of his saddle towel. Eddie towed him almost to the finish line before he realized what he was doing and took a swipe at him with his whip. The horse held on for third.

Eddie was tied up in the winner's circle taking pictures and signing autographs, and it was a while before he came back to the jocks room. Eddie always had a reputation as a scrapper and came into the jocks room saying, "Where's the rider of the three horse?" My friend, thinking he was going to have to fight his way out of the jock's room, put his helmet back on, wanting all of the protection he could get. Instead, Eddie came over and put out his hand and said, "Kid, you rode a hell of a race. You should try the big time."

I went back to the boat and set on deck smoking for a few minutes. One of the night clubs was right across the street from my boat mooring, and I could hear the band music coming across the parking lot; but I had no interest in walking over. I get up early and ten o'clock is about as late as I stay up most nights. I like sleeping on the boat, with just enough movement from passing boats to give a gentle rock that I find very soothing, and I sleep like a dead man.

When Goodman came to the barn the next morning, I gave him the printout I had gone through and told him I hadn't found anyone I thought a murderer. I had written comments alongside many names, but they weren't going to give him much help: crackpot but harmless; all business but no sense of humor; lost ball in tall weeds; a nice guy but doesn't win any races; complete horse's ass; etc.

He made a quick scan of the printout before he folded it and put it in his pocket. "Don't be discouraged about not spotting our man right away. It's is never that easy to find any kind of criminal. This guy is very good and will never stand out of the crowd. Having you look through these names may seem like a total waste of your time, but I can't pass up the opportunity to get someone who is knowledgeable with the players to take a look. If someone seemed out of place on one of these lists, we wouldn't know it. A dozen people are looking through the lives of these people, but you are the only one who knows any of them or their life style. The best I can hope for , is to have you say something like, 'what the hell was this guy doing in Chicago at this time of the year?'"

The morning went smoothly and we were finished by eleven. I was glad to go home and relax another afternoon. I ate a sandwich and took the longer printout to the couch. I was mainly curious about who would show up on this list that wasn't ex-military. The first thing that jumped out at me was the number of Jockeys on the list. There had been none on the first list, but it hadn't registered on me. It took a few minutes for me to wrap my mind around it. I would inquire about military guidelines, but evidently a guy that stood five feet four and only weighed one hundred and fifteen pounds wasn't acceptable to the service.

I started through the list line by line and didn't even finish the first page before I dozed off. When I woke up, I had a stiff neck and a bad taste in my mouth. I took a hot shower and brushed my teeth. That took the bad taste away, but I still had a stiff neck.

I started making my weekly phone calls and was involved in conversations for the rest of the day. I had two owners that I didn't particularly like, and I always saved them for last. I didn't want one of them to put me in a bad mood for the rest of my calls. The one for whom I had run the horse in Phoenix was very cool on the phone. I would even say he was icy. I recognized the signs of a man thinking of switching trainers and was very careful not to discourage that thinking. He had four horses with me and you never like to lose that many, but I didn't want to give him any reason to think I would give him special consideration in order to keep his business. He was the type that already expected special handling, and I sure wasn't going to let him think he had a hammer to use on me. I had turned down a new client a couple of weeks ago because I didn't have stall space for him, and I would let this guy go with no qualms. We ended our conversation without him admitting he was thinking of leaving, but I could tell it was on his mind.

I fell asleep again while watching Wheel of Fortune, and when I woke an hour later, I decided to just go to bed. I normally get up at five, but I came wide awake about four and didn't even feel like lying in bed. I guess I had finally reached my sleep quota. I didn't go to the barn early because I didn't want the crew to think I was sneaking in early to check up on them.

I had decided I would put one more work on the new horse and start entering him. It usually takes several entries to get a maiden in. Santa Anita uses a star system and has a lot of maidens. When you enter a horse and he doesn't draw in, he gets a star so the next time you enter him he has preference over a horse that doesn't have a star. It is not unusual to need three or four stars to get in a maiden race. I once had a maiden filly that I had entered four times and hadn't made the races yet. I was in the racing office and saw a maiden special weight race for the boys that only had ten horses. It was near the end of the meet, and I was afraid she wasn't going to get in a race before the meet was over so I entered her in the boy's race. I got in, but I caught the two best two-year olds of the year. It made me look like a total fool and I never did that again. The horse that won the race broke down later that year in the breeder's cup, and the horse that ran second went on to become "the poor man's" super horse.

I was sitting in the grandstand watching my horses when Goodman came up to talk with me. He had made a point of staying away when I was working and I knew something must be going on.

He took the seat next to me and said, "Our guy made another hit last night."

"Was it local?"

"A stock broker in Palos Verdes was found this morning in his garage with a broken neck."

"Is a stock broker rich enough to meet the wealth profile?"

"He was a partner in a brokerage and his paycheck last year was a little over eight million. It appears that someone was waiting in the garage when he came home last night."

"Did he have family at home?"

"No. He's divorced and lives alone."

"Doesn't it seem strange that this guy has so much information available to him? He knows which flight one is on and he knows that the other one is coming home late and alone."

"It's very strange, but we haven't been able to make any connections. We've worked backward on every case checking their movements for several days down to the minute. We've checked their friends and business connections and have never found any that matched up with any other case. We've been working this in every way for over two years and don't know a bit more than we did when we worked the first case. Except for the two dead grooms, we've never had the smallest clue to point us in any direction."

"Did you go to the crime scene?"

"Absolutely not. We don't know how this guy operates. If he has the crime scene under surveillance and spotted me or St. Germaine, we would not only be worthless here but might be a candidate for an ice pick along with anyone else he had seen us talking to."

"Did you by any chance check the passenger list of the plane from Hawaii for a licensed horseman?"

"No I didn't, but you can bet I'll have it checked as soon as I can make a phone call."

He took out his cell phone and walked way up in the grandstand before making the call. He talked on the phone for several minutes and left without coming back to me. I didn't know if he had gotten a lead or just figured we had said everything that needed saying.

I finished at the barn and went to the racing office to make a couple of entries without seeing him again. They only used one of the races, and I drew an outside post position, which I wasn't very happy about. I had a speed horse and wouldn't mind the outside if he was the only speed in the race, but two other speed horses were also running, and they had both drawn inside of me. It would put my horse at a disadvantage—but that's what they mean by the luck of the draw.

I had one racing this afternoon and didn't see any point in leaving and having to come back so I stopped by the kitchen for a sandwich. The boys were both there and in card games and I ate at a table with a friend and left them to their games.

While I waited for my race, I sat in my office thinking about this thing the boys had me involved in. The assassin was doing business as usual, which meant either he didn't know they were investigating him or he didn't care. I hoped it meant he didn't know, because if he knew and didn't care, he was even more dangerous than anyone was giving him credit for.

I went over for my race and lost a heartbreaker. It was very close and from the angle where I was standing it appeared that I had won. After a slight delay, the judges posted the other horse as the winner. With the modern equipment they use for photos today it is near impossible to get it wrong. I didn't even hang around to see the photo.

I went home after the race and had dinner before I resumed going through the printout. I had decided that I would try to get through one page a day. The jockeys were going to be the biggest problem because many of them were licensed in nearly every state during the year. Their agents were licensed in several states but not as many as their riders. This wasn't unusual because if a rider was based at Churchill Downs and his agent booked him to ride a stakes race in New York, the agent wouldn't go with him to New York. He would stay in Kentucky and keep booking him for the coming races there. The rider would fly up for the race and come back to Kentucky the same or next day. He would need a license to ride the race, but the agent would have booked the ride over the phone and would never have been in New York at all. He would never have needed a license.

As I went through the list, I was vaguely bothered by the fact they had excluded women. I know they had decided their killer was a man, but it still bothered me. It hadn't been too many years ago that women were nearly excluded from racing, but times have changed. Many are now involved in every aspect of racing, as trainers, jockeys, exercise riders, and grooms, and women out number the men as riders of lead the ponies. There are several of them I wouldn't want to stand toe-to-toe with in a bar fight. Of course you had to consider that the man shot in the men's restroom at the airport would have given a woman somewhat of a problem.

I finished my page and got ready for bed. I had cheated a little because I had done about a third of the page the day before. I didn't see any reason to rush because I was becoming more convinced that this was not going to produce anything of value. I told him I would go through it, but I was going to do it at my own pace.

The next morning I was giving the boys' horse his final work before I started trying to get him in a race. I worked him six furlongs from the gate and was convinced he was ready to run. He did everything right and had a decent time. I told them I would enter him in a couple of days but not to expect him to get in the first time or two I entered him.

After training, Goodman came into my office and sat down waiting for me to finish making the entries in my training log. We took great care not to discuss anything but horses when anyone was within hearing distant. Even in my office, I kept the door open and my eyes peeled for anyone near enough to overhear our conversation.

When I was finished I said, "You were on the phone a long time yesterday. Did they check the passenger list while you waited?"

"No. The office was all abuzz because we have our first link between two victims. The broker that was just killed was the broker for a man that was killed two years ago on his boat at Balboa. That points out the fact that we are so desperate that any little thing will excite us."

"Did the man in Balboa have just the one broker?"

"No. He had four or five different brokers, but he had about two hundred million with this one. He didn't have investments even near that amount with any of the others. The others were in the ten to twenty million range. I think this is a real connection."

"It sounds worth checking out."

"I guarantee you that when we finish checking this guy we will know what he had for breakfast for the last year and everyone he ever farted in front of."

"I wouldn't be surprised if you could actually do that. How about the passenger list?"

"Nothing turned up there. The only passenger on the plane with a license other than a driver's license was a private detective."

"What was a private detective doing on the plane?"

"We interviewed everyone on the plane. I read the transcript of his interview; he had been in Hawaii for a weekend vacation. I don't think he is of interest."

"That's too bad. I was hoping for something to turn up that would help us. Could I ask you something a little off of the subject? You seem to be the investigator. What is St. Germaine's part in this?"

"St. Germaine is a freak. He is the only person I ever met with a true photographic memory. He can remember everything he reads and everything he hears. He is worth more than his weight in gold to anyone he works with. I'll bet you twenty dollars that if I call him in and you name any day since we've been here that he can quote you every word you spoke in his presence on that day. And I mean word for word. I have known a lot of really smart guys over the years, but I have never met anyone that can do that. He is a true freak."

"That doesn't sound possible, but I'll take your word for it. I was just curious about his role since he never has much to say."

"He's like having a human tape recorder. On our way home at night, he repeats everything of interest he heard at his card table during the day. It's as if I sat in both games all day."

"Let me change the subject one more time. I am going to enter your horse for a race next Wednesday. It's a fifty thousand dollar maiden claiming. I don't have a clue how many entries will go in, but if the race overfills, we will most likely be excluded because we haven't entered him before and don't have a star. The only thing in our favor is that stars are only good for the exact race they were earned in. A lot of the entries for this may be dropping down from higher races and may also not have a star. In that case we all have an equal shake."

"That's great. When will you know?"

"Entries are generally two days before the race, and the draw takes place about noon on most days. I'll know as soon as the draw is over."

"That's great. I know you have a horse in this afternoon so I'll get out of your hair."

"Are you guys picking up anything of interest in the kitchen?"

"Not really; but we are getting to know a lot of people, which may serve some purpose down the road."

"How are you doing in the card game?"

"I'm up about five hundred, but I've asked St. Germaine to go easy and he is only up about a hundred."

"Why did you ask him to go easy?"

"He could be the world champion gin player if he wanted. I have played gin with him when we were just killing time and by half way through the hand he can name every card in my hand. I had him do it several time to prove it wasn't a fluke, and he never missed. He's scary with that memory of his. I didn't want him to destroy the game and run everyone off or draw attention and have people talking about us."

They left and went to the kitchen and I went to the racing office to make a couple of entries. I had better luck today and got both horses in and drew decent post positions. Waiting for the draw was a necessary evil for me, and I killed time by listening to the chatter going on between the agents.

Most of them are gamblers, which is probably what brought them to the track in the first place. They think because they are talking to the trainers all morning and visiting barns and seeing what is going on that they have better information. I suppose they do, but I promise you they don't have any better gambling luck than the regular horse player. They either don't know how to use that better information or they are really unlucky. All of the agents with good riders make great money. Their paychecks will range from two thousand to ten thousand a week, and they blow a good portion of it at the mutual windows every week. I cannot tell you how many times I have seen agents have a great week and get a check of ten thousand or better on Wednesday and come by on Saturday asking to borrow five hundred. It's an occupational hazard.

Most of the agents come to the draw even if they don't have a ride that day. They pick up mounts that other agents can't ride. If a rider is named on more than one horse in a race, he must name the horse he intends to ride. The other horse or horses that he is named on are then listed as open and need a rider. The agent that is named on the horse is supposed to have talked to the trainer beforehand and has the trainer's second choice to name on the horse. In a lot of cases, the second choice is already committed to ride another horse and isn't available either. In many cases, the agent has told the trainer he will get him the best rider available at the time. It is in fact a wild few minutes of horse trading pandemonium. Agents for some of the low-end riders only get horses that no one else will ride. Some of them are not sound and some of them just can't run. If no one names on a horse, then the stewards will name a rider. Once the draw is over, the rider named on a horse is stuck with that horse, and it is very rarely that the stewards will allow them to change. Because of the danger of being named on an unsound horse that might break down in a race, a few riders have declared they are not to be named on any horse that had not been approved by their agent before the draw. This is a good policy, but only the riders that are making a decent living can afford it. The riders that only ride one or two horses a day must ride anything they can get just to eke out a living.

If trainers would come to the draw and watch how this process actually works, I feel sure they would come to all of the draws to protect themselves. They would not believe what occurs and how they end up with the riders they get. It is the craziest system in the world, and unless you have the best horse in the race, you had better feel very lucky if you end up with a rider you approve of. What most trainers don't understand is that an agent is working for the rider and not the trainer. His job is to get the rider on the best horse in that race. If he tells you at eight o'clock that he will ride your horse and at nine o'clock someone asks him to ride a horse he thinks is better, guess what! You are out of luck and need a rider. If the agent gives you a commitment, the rules of racing oblige him to honor it, but the stewards know this rule can't be enforced. On two occasions I have seen a gung-ho steward decide to make them honor their commitments. The outcome of that effort was a draw that should take about an hour lasted all afternoon. That can't be allowed to happen because the people who do the draw have other jobs during the races. They all serve as judges of one kind or another, such as placing judge or paddock judge or claims clerk. The agents just refused to give anyone a commitment and no one had a rider, which meant that each trainer had to be contacted, and at that time of day they had already scattered all over the city and were near impossible to find. In both cases that I saw the attempt made, it only lasted one day before the stewards announced it would be business as usual.

If an agent comes to me before the draw and tells me he has to ride another horse, I don't get upset, because I have time to line up another rider. If he waits and spins me at the draw, he has a strike against him and in my game you only get two. There are enough good riders around that I don't have to put up with an agent who doesn't take care of business. I don't hold it against the rider, but I won't do business with the agent. Riders hire and fire agents from time to time, and I won't ride whichever rider that agent is working for now or in the future.

The horse I had in today was in the third race, which would still leave me part of the afternoon off. The horse belonged to the owner that I think is shopping for a new trainer, and I kind of hoped he wouldn't win. We caught an easy race and he won by daylight. The owner didn't come down to the winner's circle, and I hadn't seen him all day, so he may have not even come to the races. I didn't care one way or another. Some people are more aggravation than they are worth.

Owners sometime start thinking the trainer is an employee and that is not true. I have heard owners say a hundred times, I fired that trainer. They didn't fire anyone. They may have taken their horses away from him, but he still came to work the next morning with a business to run. I have seen trainers let an aggressive owner who likes to claim a lot of horses become such a large percentage of their business they are really hurt if that owner leaves. To make sure I don't get caught in that trap, I have a four horse limit for any one owner. If he leaves I don't miss a step and may even claim a couple of horses for myself to fill his stalls. I tell them up front when they come to me that I won't allow them to have more than four horses in my barn. Other trainers must have similar rules because it is not uncommon to see owners with horses in two or three barns at the same time. The only problem with this is if two trainers enter horses that belong to the same owner in the same race, the horses must run as a coupled entry. This can cause unnecessary problems because if a claiming race overfills, you can't run a coupled entry and one of the horses will be excluded. If one of my owners has horses with another trainer and he doesn't keep me informed where they are going to run, I may ask him to take the horses he has with me out of my barn.

I didn't feel like cooking and stopped to pick up a pizza on the way home. I sat at the table eating pizza and looking through the next page of the printout. You should never concentrate on something while you are eating because you don't realize how much you are eating. The first thing I knew I had eaten an entire large pizza and was so overstuffed I thought I was going to be sick. I didn't go to bed until ten o'clock and was still so uncomfortable I was afraid to lie down. The only good thing to come out of it was I got through three pages of the printout trying to take my mind off of the discomfort.

I normally stop for breakfast at a small coffee shop on my way to the track, but I skipped it this morning—I may never be hungry again. I saw the boys follow their horse to the track and watch him gallop. They didn't come up to where I was sitting, but when I came back to the barn, Goodman was hanging around waiting for me.

He was starting to establish a little routine. He would come into the office and take a chair and sit quietly until I was finished making entries in my training journal. He always waited for me to open the conversation.

I closed my journal and asked, "Anything new?"

"Not really. The finance people are combing through tons of paper, but the only thing they have turned up so far is that both men had huge deposits in a Dutch bank."

"I'm sure you are aware that you are looking for two very different people. The assassin is just a hired hand and is not going to have anything to do with this high finance."

He nodded his head and said, "I know that, but if we can find him we may be able to trace him to whoever is ordering the hits. You can't just look in the yellow pages for an assassin, and if we put this one out of business we may stop it temporarily. The next one may not be as good."

"I assume that while you are looking for the man with a gun, part of your taskforce is looking for the man with the money that's giving the orders."

"Yes. In fact most of them are paper pushers that are looking for the kingpin. St. Germaine and I are one of only two teams that are actually looking for the shooter. The other team is visiting the police departments in every city where a hit was made. They are looking at the evidence that's been gathered and searching for anything that might have been overlooked. They are interviewing the detectives that worked the crime scenes and talking to their crime lab people. We are leaving no stone unturned."

"I find it hard to believe that a man who is impulsive enough to walk into a men's restroom in one of the busiest airports in the country and shoot someone to death has left no clues whatsoever in a dozen murders."

"I can understand how you feel, but let me give you an example of how thorough this guy is. We recovered a footprint from the dust on the floor of the garage in Palos Verdes. The foot print was made by a Nike tennis shoe called Classic. It was size nine. The shooter in the men's room at LAX had stepped in a damp spot on the floor. Because we got there right away we were able to get a partial print. It was a size nine tennis shoe but made by Converse. The guy even wears different shoes every time, and I will bet he destroys them afterwards. The only thing we know is he wears a size nine shoe. That narrows it down to only ten million people."

"I understand the point you're making, but I'm still hung up on him shooting a man in the men's room of the airport. That doesn't seem to be the cool and calculating guy you're describing. I don't get it. To top it off, he was seen there by people who knew him—if you are right about the grooms. It doesn't make sense to me. Tell me what I'm missing."

"I have to admit that this was the first time he ever put himself in danger of exposure. We think that might be the reason he took the extra precaution of killing the grooms—just because they had seen him at the airport. Everyone working this case agrees this hit had something special about it; it had to be a rush job because he has never acted like a cowboy before. The paper pushers are looking into the man's affairs, trying to find something that was coming up in the near future that was important enough to have him killed over. Things like that take a long time to dig out, but we have hopes."

"I would think the airport has surveillance cameras everywhere. Can't you see him going in or coming out of the rest room?"

"We had to have a court order before the airport could turn over the tapes to us. It's only in the movies they can just give them to you. We've only had them a couple of days and there are hundreds of them. We are looking at them as we speak, but it could take several days. We don't expect a homerun because it was raining that day, and most people had raincoats and hats on. If he had on a hat and kept his head down, we can't get much even when we spot him."

I didn't have a horse in today and couldn't face the printout waiting for me at home. I walked over to the kitchen thinking I would eat lunch and maybe play cards for a couple of hours. I was still not very hungry even though I had missed breakfast, but I had a sandwich. Half a dozen games were in progress, and it wasn't long before a player quit and the others asked me to play. It was a good game, and I played a little longer than I had intended; but I finally had to admit that the printout would still be there no matter how long I played. I couldn't dodge the fact that it would wait for me no matter what.

I had dinner and tackled the printout, but it was a struggle. I forced myself to do a full page, but I had to keep backing up and going over parts of it again. I would realize I had read ten names without a single one registering on my brain. This was some kind of new torture the FBI had dreamed up. To stop the pain, I was supposed to confess that I was the hit man.

I went to bed and had a dream about some nut in Speedos and cowboy boots chasing me with an ice pick. I woke up in the morning exhausted. That really ticked me off because I had two horses in this afternoon and wouldn't have time to get a nap.

One of the horses I am running today belongs to me. He will probably be the favorite and has a good chance to win. There is also a good chance he will be claimed. He won the same race two weeks ago with several of the same horses in it. He is an honest horse that gives his best every time you send him over. As long as you run him where he belongs, he is always going to be tough to beat. I kind of hate to lose him, but I don't hate it enough to run him where he can't win.

The boys were at the barn but didn't have much to say, so I assumed nothing new had happened. They hung around until their horse went to the track and then went to the kitchen to play cards. I was glad they went away without a lot of conversation because I wasn't in the mood. So far the distractions they were causing me hadn't interfered with my business activities, but I still wanted to keep it to a minimum. I didn't think this was going to help them catch their man and didn't intend for it to disrupt my life.

I got through the morning without any problems and went to the racing office to enter a horse and wait for the draw. My horse drew the six hole, which wasn't a bad spot. It was a route race and post position is not very important, but I always hate to be way outside.

I stopped at the kitchen on the way back and ate lunch. The boys were both in games and I didn't think they even saw that I was there. St. Germaine seemed to be in deep conversation with one of the players at his table. He appeared to be asking a lot of questions about whatever it was that had caught his interest. They wouldn't dare let anyone know what their interest actually was, so it was probably something about horses or horseracing.

I went back to the barn and read the last three days of the Racing Form while I waited for time to take my first horse over. This is the worst time of a race. You don't have time to go anywhere and you don't have anything to do. It's like being in jail. I save my forms for this time to give me something to read. I'm not interested in betting on the horses so I only read for the news and to follow the charts, looking for a horse that might be a good claim.

When I arrived at the saddling paddock, the paddock judge informed me that my rider had taken a fall in the preceding race and I needed a rider. He gave me a list of the riders in the room without a mount that were willing to ride my horse. Fortunately a couple of the better riders had put their name on the list. They almost never do that because usually they have planned their day down to the last glass of water and aren't willing to disrupt it by picking up a horse they had not planned to ride.

I chose the one I had the most history with, because the better the relationship you have with the rider the more he will trust what you tell him about the horse. We were delayed in the paddock for a minute or two while the new rider put on the right colors and got ready to ride. As soon as the rider came into the paddock, the judge called riders up so I really didn't have time to talk to him. I led him to the track and barely had time to tell him that the horse likes to lay close to the leaders before the pony rider took him from me. That's racing luck—and at least I had a solid rider. In these situations you can end up with a rider that doesn't ride enough decent horses to even know where the winners circle is.

The rider rode a good race, but not knowing the horse very well, he went to the lead a little early. I thought he was going to get run down in the stretch, but he hung on to win by a head. As I suspected he was claimed. The trainer that took him a habit of laying the horse up for a couple of months and then running him back at a lower price than he claimed him for. This scares a lot of people off. They think something is wrong with the horse and are afraid to claim him. He steals a lot of races that way. But since I know the horse is sound, that's not going to work with me. If he runs him back cheaper, I'll own him again.

I was in jail again, with an hour and a half to wait for my next race. I didn't have anything to read so I walked to the kitchen and watched the card games for a while. The kitchen has TV monitors for the horsemen to watch the races. There was no danger of the time getting away from me because I could see the races in progress.

A couple of friends offered congratulations on my win, and someone I didn't know very well offered condolences on losing the horse. I thought he was fishing for information on whether it had been a good claim or not. I couldn't say it had been a bad claim and then claim him right back without looking like a horse's ass, so I just shrugged my shoulders and said I knew they were going to claim him. I was telling him that I knew the horse was going to be claimed, but I didn't scratch him to save him. I would let him draw his own conclusions about what I thought of the horse.

I couldn't work up any enthusiasm for the last race. It was an allowance race with two heavy hitters in it. I didn't think I had any chance of outrunning either one of them and I didn't. I barely hung on for third in a close photo and was glad my day was over. The horse came out of the race with a cut in the coronet band that looked as if he had been stepped on. It wasn't too bad and the groom assured me he could take care of it without the vet. I examined it carefully and decided he was right. I left him with it and went on home.

On the way home I argued with myself about the printout. I had vowed to do at least one page per day, but I didn't have the energy for it today. In the end I was saved by the telephone. It was an old friend who had relocated to Texas when they started racing there. He was in town for the horses of racing age auction coming up this weekend and wanted to get together for a drink. I was happy to oblige and agreed to meet him in an hour.

I had fully intended to be in bed by nine, but I knew that time table was shot to hell. My friend is living proof that gossip is not limited to the female gender. He talked nonstop for three hours about every person we both knew. I felt as if I had been there for all of these past five or six years. He didn't leave out a single thing about the lives and loves and divorces of every person he even thought I might know. Some of it was entertaining and some of it was sad to hear, but none of it was boring. He told me that a few of the guys were in town for the sale and I should come and say hello. I let him think that I had allowed him to persuade me to attend the sale, but I never miss them if at all possible.

Only about three auctions take place each year in Southern California and all of the breeders and a large portion of the owners always attend. I am not looking for new clients at the present time, but it is a great opportunity to renew old friendships with people who don't frequent the racetrack but are very much involved with Thoroughbred horses. At these auctions you have a chance to meet old friends and make new friends, and it is two days of relaxing and enjoying the company of horsemen from all aspects of the business. I feel better about the industry as a whole after a couple of days of these gatherings.

It finally reached the point that I had to tap my watch and remind him I wasn't on vacation like him. He apologized for running off at the mouth for so long, and I invited him to come out to the track in the morning. Actually I was relieved when he told me he had one of his owners flying in for the sale, and he needed to pick him up at the airport. I agreed to have a drink with him and his owner at the sale and went home.

The next morning I called the boys into the office and said, "There is an auction this weekend, and there will be a couple of thousand horsemen attending. You might find it interesting, providing you don't run into anyone you know."

Goodman asked, "What kind of horsemen?"

"Every type of horseman from the wealthiest to the poorest: breeders, bloodstock agents, owners, trainers, and many of their employees. Even some horse equipment vendors will set up as well as most of the van lines."

"I can't imagine that we will run into anyone we know, but if we do we have a racehorse as a hobby, and it has nothing to do with our business."

"I understand that, but I don't think it would help your investigation if the word got around that you are FBI."

"I don't think that will happen, but we will be very cautious and on the alert for anyone who might know us."

We left it at that, and I went through my normal morning routine. They went to the kitchen after their horse finished his training, and I didn't see them the rest of the day. It started raining about ten o'clock and appeared to be a day-long affair. I had a horse in the last race that couldn't stand up in the mud. When it was still raining steadily at two o'clock, I went over and scratched him and went home.

I had a late lunch or an early dinner—depending on how I felt later—and settled down with the printout. There were a lot of people on the list that I didn't know personally, but only a handful that I didn't at least know who they were. Each time I ran across one that had been licensed at places I had been at the same time, I spent extra time trying to remember them and in some cases did.

I finished my page, and even though it was still early, I had no intention of starting a new one. The more names I looked over the more I was convinced this was a total waste of my time. If the guy is as covert as they are claiming, I'm sure he is taking great care to not appear on many lists. I watched a dumb police program for an hour and went to bed.

I awoke early and for the first time in several days felt rested. I stopped for breakfast on my way to the barn and was surprised to find the boys already there when I arrived.

As I unlocked my office, I said to Goodman, "You guys are really getting into the early morning routine of the racetrack."

"It's an occupational hazard of the Bureau. The people doing the research are on the East Coast and are way ahead of us in time zones. They think nine o'clock there means nine o'clock all over the world. They don't care that it's not even daylight here."

"Do they call you every morning?"

"The task force coordinator does. He thinks we need to file a report every morning about our progress. I'm starting to think he expects us to find a guy walking around the track with a sign on his back that says assassin for hire. He is starting to get on my nerves. He did relay one thing of interest this morning. The LAX victim was scheduled to make an announcement in a few days of a tender offer. It was for a mid-sized pump manufacturer that ordinarily wouldn't get our attention. The company is in financial trouble, and their main plant is in foreclosure. The thing that rang our bell is the lender that is foreclosing is the same Dutch bank that we found linked to two previous victims."

"Wow, that's a coincidence."

"One link is a coincidence. Two is a solid lead. They will put these guys under a very powerful microscope."

"How do you prosecute a bank for murder?"

"That's not my problem, but they'll figure something out if the bank proves to be the assassin's employer. As of now it's only a lead."

I had a busy morning ahead and I sent their horse to the track in the first group to insure they didn't hang around. They were starting to get too familiar and be kind of in the way. I understood this was new for them and they were trying to soak up as much knowledge as possible, but I didn't have time to answer every little question. I discouraged my regular owners from doing this and didn't see any reason to treat them any differently. If anything, they deserved less of my time because this wasn't going to be a permanent relationship.

I had several horses to work and one I had to send to the gate to get an OK to run in blinkers. I don't run as many horses in blinkers as most trainers. Many trainers run nearly all of their horses in blinkers, and I don't see anything wrong with that, but I don't think it's necessary. I am putting blinkers on this horse because he seems to be intimidated by other horses, and I thought it might help if he couldn't see them. I only try blinkers when I think they might be of some use.

I don't do several things that are automatic with many trainers. I don't run many of my horses in leg wraps because I have decided that the injuries caused by carelessly applied wraps outweigh the little bit of extra support they provide. I am the only trainer I know that doesn't tie the tongue of every horse he runs. I stopped doing that a couple of years ago and found that my win percentage didn't go down at all. I only tie their tongue now if the rider convinces me the horse needs it for some reason. Some trainers drape every piece of equipment on a horse they can find, but I think it is more of an aggravation to both the horse and the trainer than it is worth. In most cases a saddle and a bridle are my total race equipment.

I was working three sets of three this morning. Race riders come out in the morning to work horses they are going to ride or horses that are in a barn for which they ride a lot of horses. I try to use my exercise riders instead of race riders. One reason is that race riders tend to work them too fast. I gallop my horses faster than most trainers, but I work them slower. I am not interested in testing a horse every time I send him to the track for a work. Another reason is that if a rider works a horse for you, he expects to ride him in his next race. This can cause unnecessary bad feelings between you and the riders. Agents arrange a rider's mounts and most of the time riders have no idea how they came to be on one horse and not another. If a rider works a horse two or three times for you and on race day you have another rider on the horse, he has no idea that his agent told you he couldn't ride the horse because he already had a mount in that race. The rider thinks you didn't ride him after he had worked him for you and is steamed about it. I like the freedom of not being committed to any rider with any horse. I can get the best rider that is available on that particular day without causing any animosity.

At the beginning of a meet, riders looking for business are a nuisance. Six or eight of them come by every morning offering to work horses for you. They think if you will let them work a few, you will feel obligated to ride them some. It usually takes two or three weeks for them to give up and stop bugging you every morning. They are trying to make a living, and I would never insult them; I just hold firm to my no thanks reply.

I had a set in mid-stretch of a work when the starter broke my blinker horse out of the gate. I hadn't been watching closely, and he got away without my starting a watch on him. I would have to take the clocker's time on him. I didn't like to do that because the clocker's time is unreliable. They do the best they can, but the job can be overwhelming. It is not unusual to have ten or twelve horses working at the same time and breaking from different poles on the track. It is impossible for only two or three people to get an accurate time on them all. I time all of my horses, and it is not unusual for the time that gets published to be faster by four or five seconds than they truly went. When they miss a horse, they make an educated guess, and it happens a lot. The only bad thing about it is some gamblers give workouts much more importance than they actually are. Even if the time is accurate, it has very little bearing on the horse's racing ability.

With so many to work, they were running behind at the barn and my last horse didn't come off the track until about ten minutes before they closed it for training. I like to make my notes while they are fresh in my mind, so I sat a few minutes finishing before I started for the barn. I was running a little late and decided to stop by the racing office and make my entries before I went to the barn. I would come back for the draw, but I wanted to get my entries in before they started calling races off that didn't have enough horses to use. I also wanted to pick up a catalog for the auction. They always drop off several cartons in the racing office for the trainers.

Instead of the printouts, tonight I would peruse the catalog. There might be something of interest in the sale. You never know when there will be a sleeper that is worth a gamble.

A friend of mine had bought a four-year-old horse in the racing age sale in New York for three thousand dollars. The horse had never started, and he didn't know a thing about him but liked his looks. As soon as he was training good, he entered him in a bottom maiden claiming race. He worked him before going to the racing office to make the entry and hung around the office waiting for the clocker to post the workouts. The track where he was racing was deep and slow and the winning times for six furlong races were one thirteen to one fourteen. The clocker came out and hung the day sheet, and the time on his horse was one ten flat. He stormed into the clocker's office demanding to know why he had posted such a crazy time. The clocker assured him that he had personally clocked him and the time was accurate.

Once you make an entry, you can't take it back; but he was in luck because the maiden claiming was overfilling, and a maiden special weight they were trying to make go needed a couple of horses. They let him take his horse out of the cheap race and move him to the special weight. He won the race by several lengths and the trainer entered him right back in a non-winners of two allowance race. When he also won this race easily, everyone started to pay attention. In the meantime a friend had looked the horse up for him and found that the horse had outstanding breeding and sold three years ago at the yearling sale for four hundred thousand dollars. Since he had never started, he had to have a serious problem; but it had not shown up as yet and didn't seem to affect his running. He entered him in a non-winner of three allowance race, which he also won by about three lengths. A bloodstock agent made an offer of three hundred thousand dollars, which he promptly accepted. It was the first real money he had ever had, and I was happy for him.

I took three catalogs in case the boys wanted one and went back to the barn. The crew had coped with the heavy morning and was finishing up in good order. I transferred my notes into my training log and went back to the racing office to wait for the draw.

The normal group of agents and two or three trainers were hanging around swapping stories. One group was talking about Secretariat and one of the trainers said, "You can bet if I had Secretariat he would never have won the Triple Crown."

One of the agents asked, "Are you telling us you are a bad trainer?"

"No. I'm telling you if I had him I would have gotten him eligible for starter allowances and killed the world with him."

This broke everyone up and was the best joke of the day. If you won every starter allowance in the country, you might win two hundred thousand dollars. That wouldn't pay Secretariat's insurance policy for one year. But oddly enough he might have really done just that. Trainers think in weird ways.

I had entered three horses and got the weenie. They didn't use two of my races and my horse was excluded in the other one. I went back to the barn and found the crew had finished their work and disappeared. I finished a few things in the office and went to the kitchen for lunch.

Goodman and St. Germaine were both in card games and I didn't bother them. I would give them catalogs when they came to the barn in the morning. I had lunch and sat talking to a trainer I had known for a long time. He wasn't having a good meet and was thinking of taking his horses to Chicago. He thought they would fit better there and was probably right. You need to run where your horses are competitive and can win races or you can't make any money. Owners think your day rate is making you rich, but it barely pays the expenses, and most of the time doesn't even do that. The only profit is your ten percent of the purse money. No wins, no profit.

When the trainer left, I went home to go over the sale catalog. I went through every horse carefully but only found four horses that I was mildly interested in. I wasn't very enthused about any of them, but I would inspect the four before they went into the ring. Most of the horses that come to this sale are not racing material or the owners could have found a customer. Decent horses are always in demand and not enough of them are on the market. If they are for sale with no buyers, it's because they are way overpriced. Since you are buying as is in the sale ring with no guarantees, they go very cheap, and sometimes you are willing to take the risk and try one.

I went to bed and read until I was falling asleep, which didn't take very long. I awoke with a start when my alarm went off and for a minute couldn't think where I was. I don't know what caused my confusion, but I felt groggy and didn't start to feel normal until I had stopped at the restaurant and had breakfast.

I arrived at the barn a few minutes late and my assistant had already sent three horses to the track. I went up to watch them, but they were finished by the time I made it to the track. I wasn't upset because I missed them; we have a lot of work to get done every morning and the world doesn't stop turning because of me.

We had worked so many yesterday that would just walk today we had an easy morning. By nine o'clock we were finished with all of the horses that were going to the track. I made my notes and was ready to go to the sale by ten. I had worked the horses the day before to free me up to get out early. I was surprised that the boys didn't show up and took the two extra catalogs with me. If they came to the auction, I would have catalogs for them in case they happened to run short at the sale.

As I drove into the parking lot, I was impressed by the number of cars. If this was any indication, they should have a good sale. I had to park a mile away and walk, but it was a beautiful day and I was looking forward to spending the day visiting with friends. It was made even better because I didn't have any business on my agenda and could just visit.

They always set up a huge tent as a sales pavilion, and the first people I met when I walked in were the boys. They were standing together by the entrance watching the people coming in and looking as if they didn't know what to do next.

Goodman smiled when he saw me enter and said something to St. Germaine, who was facing the other way. They came over to meet me and Goodman said, "I didn't know what time you would get here."

"Have you guys looked around any?"

"No. We were afraid if we missed you we might not find you all day. There are a lot of people here."

"Did you get a catalog yet?"

"No. We haven't left this spot since we came."

"Let's go in the stable area and we can stop at the sales office and pickup catalogs for you. I have a couple extra in the truck if they are out."

The sales office was the first building behind the pavilion, and they still had a few catalogs although they were getting short. We walked through the stable area not looking at anything in particular; I was just letting them take in the whole experience. I spoke to a few friends in passing but didn't stop to talk to any. When horsemen are inspecting horses is not the time to have friendly chats. That would come later when they were not busy.

One of the horses on my list was out of his stall being shown to a prospective buyer. It was a perfect time to look him over without having to engage in a dialog with the agent. I liked his conformation, but as I walked around him I saw that he had a bad suspensory ligament. I have never had any luck with horses that had bowed tendons or a blown suspensory. I passed on this one. He wasn't my kind of gamble.

We walked through the stable area and stopped to watch whenever a horse was being shown. The boys were seeing a part of the horse industry that I find fun, and they were soaking it up like sponges. By the time they finished this gig, they might become lifelong horsemen. They were male versions of Alice in Wonderland.

Two barns over I found another of the horses I had marked on my list. This was a filly out of a mare that I had trained and really liked. I had to ask the agent to take her out, which meant I had to listen to his sales pitch. She was larger than I had expected. Her mother had been on the small side but was an honest runner. I looked her over and didn't find anything that would make her un-buyable. She had made four starts without breaking her maiden, which would turn off the buyers and make her very cheap. Her feet were a total mess, and I suspected that whoever had been training her, tried to be his own farrier. She showed every sign of poor care and might have never had a chance. I didn't mark her off, and for the right price I might take a flier.

The next horse had been scratched out of the sale. Either he had been sold beforehand or had injured himself. It's not uncommon to have a horse get cut or banged up on the way to the sale and be scratched. The last horse on my list was the one I was most interested in. He had been a good allowance horse as a two-year-old and had disappeared. The word around the track was he had been operated on for a chip in his knee. He was now four and worth a look.

As we entered the barn he was in, we ran into an old owner of mine. He saw me and came over to say hello. He looked to be the definitive man of means: well dressed in expensive casual cloths and well groomed with short, styled hair. He had a round baby face that made him appear to be thirty when I knew he was more like fifty.

I introduced him to the boys and we talked for a few minutes. I told him I would catch up with him in the pavilion, and we would spend some time together. As he turned to leave I said, "You're looking good, Dudley, don't leave before we have time to visit."

When he was out of earshot, Goodman said, "Is his name really Dudley?"

I laughed and said, "It's a nickname that a lady friend of ours hung on him. She called him Dudley do Right because he is a total screw-up. He comes from money and has dedicated his life to wasting it in every way he can. If you look in the dictionary under weird, you'll see his picture. He's the sort of person you're looking for except he can't tie his shoe laces and can't be depended on for anything."

"What do you mean by weird?"

"I'll give you an example of the sort of things that are normal for him. He and I went to Hawaii for a vacation. The first day we were there we met a girl from Georgia who was a radio station executive of some kind. She was there for a convention and Dudley fell in love. He put a rush on her that would have made Mother Theresa succumb. He met her for breakfast every morning and took up every spare minute she had available. He must have spent several hundred dollars at the bar on her. She kept putting him off and going to convention meetings every time he tried to get her alone. On her last night, he invited her to go out with us in the evening. She told him she had to go to the awards banquet but would meet us afterwards. She didn't show up where he had arranged for her to meet us, and since we had been drinking more or less all day we gave up and went back to our room. I had just gone to bed and Dudley was undressing to go to bed when the phone rang. The phone was on a table that was between the beds and I answered it. The voice on the other end said, 'This is Sara. I'm sorry the banquet ran so late. I just got in. Why don't you come on up. I'm in room 612 just above your room.'

"I said, 'Whoa, you've got the wrong stud honey, hold on a minute,' and handed the phone to Dudley.

"He talked to her for a minute or two and ended by saying, 'I'll be right up.' He handed the phone back to me to hang up and finished undressing and went to bed. I have seen him pull similar stunts on numerous occasions. He is all about the chasing and not the catching."

"I agree that's weird, but what do you mean by comes from money?"

"I think his parents were well off but I never met them. His grandmother, who lived in Texas, had the money and bailed him out on a regular basis. He swapped cars like I swapped shirts. Every time he showed up he would have a new car and they were expensive types. I remember a Porsche and a Lotus just to name a couple. Every time he got in over his head, he would take off for Texas, and when he came back everything was all right again.

"He was the one who got me into my sailboat. He showed up one day and wanted me to go look at boats with him. He had decided to buy a sail boat and wanted to go shopping. We looked at boats every afternoon for a month. We finally decided that we had found the most boat for the best price, and he was negotiating for price on the basis we were going to buy two. I had got into the spirit of the thing and agreed to buy one. We put down our deposits, but when the boats came, he didn't take his. That was just another example of how undependable he was—and is. You can't count on him for the smallest or the most important thing. He couldn't care less what it matters to you. He might be interested this morning but by afternoon has forgotten about it and doesn't want to be bothered. If you try to scold him for something he did or did not do, he just doesn't come around for a month or two, thinking you will have forgotten about it. I don't forget things like that and about the last thing he ever said to me was I never met anyone who holds a grudge like you do. That was when I ran into him in a bar about a month after he left me stranded in Tahiti on a trip he had planned for us and then didn't show up."

We found the last horse on my list, and they had him out of the stall. Three or four obviously interested parties were looking at the colt when we walked up. A dozen people were gathered around and it was hard to tell who was with whom. I knew two of the trainers who were looking him over and just nodded at them by way of saying hello. They had the handler jog him up and down the shed row until I began to think they were going to wear him out. The horse was traveling sound and square, but that didn't mean he would stand up under training.

We went back to the pavilion tent and were standing at the bar getting drinks when the loud speaker announced that Hiram Jordan had a phone call in the office. I laughed and said, "Nothing ever changes."

"What's funny about that announcement?"

"That's Hiram's method of cheap advertisement. To keep his name in everyone's mind and to make it appear that he is a busy wheeler-dealer, he'll call and have himself paged six or eight times today. He's done that for years."

I saw four trainers I knew from Texas grouped in the far corner of the pavilion with six strangers, who I assumed were their owners. That was way too much introducing to be done, so I asked the boys to excuse me for a minute and walked over alone. They all had drinks in hand and by the tone of their conversation, I was sure this wasn't the first round. They were having a good time and didn't seem to mind that I didn't join them. They made me promise to go to dinner after the sale, but I wasn't sure they would remember inviting me.

They were getting ready to start the sale, and I suggested the boys take a seat and watch for awhile. I explained that these were horses that had been tried and found lacking or were not sound or just didn't measure up for whatever reason. I told them not to expect any earth-shattering prices and to just watch the action and the people and to not wave at anyone unless they wanted to end up owning another horse. I was going to circulate among the people outside the tent and visit a little with old friends. As I left I saw them sit down in the back row.

The first person I met when I walked out of the tent was Mandy. She was waiting for me and greeted me with a big smile and a quick kiss. I had taken her out after the last two auctions and she made me promise to take her sailing the next afternoon. This was the strangest situation I had ever been involved in. I had seen her at every auction for the last four or five years but had never had much to say to her. We had spoken several times when we happened to be standing together looking at horses, but nothing personal ever transpired. A couple of years ago I had brought a girl that exercised horses for me to the sale, and all of a sudden Mandy was everywhere I went. She asked me about my opinion of horses that were selling and everything else she could think of to start a conversation. She must have approached me a dozen times during the day. The girl I was with was miffed by the end of the day. The second day of the sale I came alone, and Mandy was ever present the entire day. I took her out after the sale and we had a great time. I don't know where she is from or what she does the rest of the year. I only see her at the auctions and we have dated afterwards ever since. It's like the movie "Same Time Next Year." I asked her what brought about the change in her, and she said since I had never hit on her, she couldn't be sure I wasn't gay until she saw me with a date.

I moved around among the horsemen, visiting with first one and then another. The theme among horse trainers always seems to be gloom and doom. They complain to each other about bad owners and bad horses. The owners always expect more than they are willing to pay for, and the horses always manage to run a bad race the day you bet your money on them. I could agree about the owners, but I am one of those rare trainers who are not willing to push their money through the mutual windows, so the complaint about bad races doesn't affect me as much.

I listened to a bloodstock agent who was doing a juggling act with an owner. He was trying to tout him on a horse he had in the sale and at the same time was trying to get him to put a price on a horse the prospect owned that the agent had a buyer for. It didn't sound good for the agent. The owner didn't like the horse the agent was selling, and his horse wasn't for sale.

The filly was coming into the ring soon so I walked to the entry at the back of the pavilion where they bring the horses into the ring. They have a spotter back there so you can bid without going into the tent. There wasn't much interest in her, and I bought her for sixteen hundred dollars. I would get her straightened out and give her a shot. If she didn't work out, she had some value as a broodmare prospect or a saddle horse. I couldn't lose too much—it was worth a chance.

The colt wouldn't be for a couple of hours so I went in to see how the boys were doing. They were near the bar talking to some people and didn't even notice me. I hung around a few minutes and went back outside to continue visiting.

I called my friend at Pomona to ask if he was interested in taking the filly for me and maybe another horse if I should get him bought. He not only was interested but offered to hook up his trailer and pick them up for me. We settled on a price and I told him I would call him after the other horse sold and let him know if it was one or two.

I meandered through the barn area and ended back at the barn where the colt was stabled. Nobody was looking now, and they were shining him up to take him to the sale ring. I liked him more the second time and was impressed with how quietly he stood while two people were rubbing him down with their shine towels. He seemed to be very levelheaded and sensible. I hoped with all of the interest in him he wasn't going to be too expensive. I made a mental note to myself that I wouldn't give more than six thousand for him and vowed to stick to it.

I ran into a groom who had worked for me two or three different times. He was working for a trainer in San Francisco and liked it up there. He is typical of a lot of grooms who like to move around. They never seem to stay committed to one place or one trainer. He was a good groom, but he had left me the last time in the middle of a race day over some silly argument he had with another groom. I would never hire him again but still liked him as a person.

The colt would be coming up in half an hour so I went back to the pavilion to get a spot in the back. They brought him while I was talking to an owner from Phoenix who had bought three already. He was shopping in the two thousand dollar range, hoping to get something that could compete at the bottom there. He asked if I knew anything about this colt and I told him no. I didn't know anything for sure about him and wasn't going to repeat rumors.

They led the colt into the ring and some big spender made an opening bid of five hundred dollars. It must have scared everyone to death because it was a minute or two before they got another bid. I was afraid they would hammer him down for the five hundred before someone finally bid a thousand. They had a couple of bidders up to the three thousand mark and the bidding stalled. I waited until I felt they were about to sell him and held up four fingers. I didn't want to bid five hundred and let the other bidder back in for another five hundred. I wanted him to realize that I was serious and he wasn't going to steal him. I was surprised when the other bidder didn't come back and I got him for the four.

I called the trainer from Pomona and his wife said he had already hooked up his trailer and was on his way. I went to the office and paid for my purchases and got the release slips, so we were ready to load and go as soon as he arrived. I didn't think that would be too long so I walked to the stable gate to wait for him. It's a good thing I didn't fool around because he pulled in the gate about ten minutes later.

I went for the filly first because I figured she might be the hardest to load, and I was right. She gave us trouble in every way. It was plain that she had not been handled very much by anyone very skillful. I couldn't believe that a filly that had four starts on the racetrack was barely broke to lead. Whoever had this filly had just brought her in from the farm and entered her in a race. She had never had a chance and I hoped she wasn't ruined.

The colt was just the opposite. He was a dream to handle and walked in the trailer like he was a show horse that was loaded every week to go to a horse show. If he couldn't run, I would make a pony horse of him. He was levelheaded enough to be anything you wanted a horse to be.

I went back to the pavilion and found the boys gone. The sale was winding down for the day. With just a few horses left to sell today, most of the people had cleared out, and the tent was nearly empty. My friend from Texas was waiting for me and came over the minute I entered the tent.

"I was afraid you had forgotten about dinner and left."

"No. I bought a couple of cheap horses and had to get them loaded and on the road."

"Did you get anything decent?"

"At the prices I paid for these things, they can't be very much. I just wanted something to play with."

"Where do you suggest we eat?"

"The area around Hollywood Park is not very desirable anymore. Where are you guys staying?"

"We are near the airport."

"I think the best bet would be one of the restaurants at Marina Del Ray."

"That sounds fine to me. Pick one out and we'll meet you there."

"Most of them have bands and you can't hear yourself think. How about Charlie Brown's?"

"That works for me. Are you finished with your business?"

"Yes. I'm ready to leave anytime you are."

"The guys are in the sales office. I'll round them up and we're on our way."

"How many will there be? I'll capture us a spot."

"There will be six of us and you. Some of the owners have their wives with them and can't go drinking with the boys."

"They will probably save a lot of money. I'll see you there."

I drove over to the marina and gave my keys to the valet. I have so much paper work in my truck I always hate to leave it in valet parking, but if you don't want to hire a cab to get you from where you parked to the restaurant, you have to use valet parking.

I went in and was happy to see it wasn't crowded yet. I picked a table with a few vacant tables around it and started pushing three of them together. The waitress came over with a quizzical look on her face to see what I was doing. I was glad I knew her, and she left me alone after I explained the group was on its way.

They came in two cars, the first group arriving in about ten minutes. We had ordered the first round of drinks before the second group came. After everyone was settled, the conversation became a mixed bag of people all talking at one time and lapses of silence when no one was talking. Two guys sitting together would be talking to each other and two guys at separate ends of the table would be talking together. It was easy to see they all were way ahead of me in their drinking. None of them was drunk but none of them was sober either. The conversation bounced all over the globe.

One of the trainers that I hadn't seen in many years said, "I don't know why I should even be talking to you. I am still mad about you costing me the training title that time."

One of the other trainers asked, "How did he cost you a training title?"

"It was the last week of the meet and I was tied for leading trainer. I had never won a training title before and really wanted it. I had saved two fillies that I was sure would win. I ran one on Monday and one on Saturday, and this nimrod beat me both times with the same horse. The other trainer won a race on Saturday and beat me by one."

I laughed and said, "That was fifteen years ago; you can't still be mad."

"I'll still be mad the day I die."

"Well, it won't make any difference then if I rub salt in the wound and tell you how I came to run a horse twice in a week. The filly belonged to me, and I ended up one stall short when I got to the meet. I took her to a boarding stable that was down the street from the track. I went over after training every day and put her on the hot walker while I cleaned her stall. That's all of the exercise she had for two months. Two weeks before the meet was over, I shipped two horses to California and brought her over. I galloped her the first day, and worked her on the second day. I entered her two days later, and when she won I decided to enter her right back. She had two months off and I didn't think a quick back would knock her out. I didn't expect her to win the second time—I was just hoping for part of it. I would have been happy with a third or fourth."

"You didn't beat my two good fillies with a horse that hadn't trained in two months. You're just pulling my leg."

"I swear to God that's what happened."

"Don't you ever tell my wife that story. She was more upset than I was and would probably attack you with her purse."

The talk droned on for two hours and several rounds of drinks before something came up that caught my attention. One of the trainers said, "I saw Jodi Breaux was named on a horse yesterday. Is she riding here on a regular basis?"

"Well, according to an article in the Form at the beginning of the meet, she was moving her tack here from New York, but you can't prove it by me. She has only ridden three or four horses the entire meet and I have never seen her anywhere on the track."

"How about her agent? Have you seen him at all?"

"I have no idea who her agent is, and no one has ever spoken to me about riding her."

"I rode her in a stakes race last fall, and I have to tell you it was the strangest experience I ever had."

"Strange in what way?"

"To begin with it took me a week to get in touch with her agent. I called four days in a row before he finally called me back. I would have blown him off after the second call, but the horse belongs to a lady that insisted she must have this girl ride her horse. I have never seen her ride, but she has had a decent career in New York, so I figured it would be alright. When he finally returned my call, I couldn't get him to commit one way or the other. He wouldn't say yes and he wouldn't say no. It was a two hundred thousand dollar stakes race for fillies, and I had the heavy favorite. Most agents would jump at the chance to get their rider in that spot, but he stalled me off, saying he would let me know in a couple of days. I had to bite my tongue to keep from telling him where he should spend those couple of days."

"Did he ride the horse?"

"I told the lady who owns the horse I was having trouble getting her agent to take the mount. The lady saw that Jodi was named on a horse the next day and called the jocks room at the track and talked to Jodi in person. I could never have gotten away with that, but this lady is very pushy. It turns out the agent is her husband. She apologized for his actions and promised to ride the horse. The bad thing about it was he never did call me back. I named her on the horse and was on pins and needles waiting to see if she showed up"

"Did she show?"

"She blew in about eleven o'clock and barely had time to get licensed before she had to be in the room. Her husband was with her and never said a word to me or anyone else. I guess he was pissed off about the lady going around him. She rode a good race and the filly won easy so everything worked out, but it was a ticklish situation. The husband was standing at the rail of the winners circle, and she went over and kissed him after they took the pictures. My wife asked who he was and wondered why he didn't come in for the win picture.

They must have spent the night because my wife saw him the next day in a discount shoe store buying a dozen pairs of tennis shoes. They must not have discount shoes in New York."

"Did she ask him about it?"

"No. She was in the women's section and saw him at the checkout with his shopping cart full of tennis shoes. He didn't see her, and she only recognized him from the day before at the winners circle. She only mentioned it to me because he looked so strange buying a whole shopping cart full of shoes."

"I have never met the man. What's his name?"

"I don't remember off hand. I think it was John Mueller or something like that, and he spoke with a slight accent."

"You're from Texas. Anyone without a drawl has a strange accent to you. Just out of curiosity, how come the owner insisted on Jodi as the rider?"

"This is a strange lady. She is extremely wealthy and although she has been married two or three times, I think she is a closet dike. She only wants girls to handle her horses, and I have to keep a female groom on the payroll to take care of her three horses. She thinks girls will treat her horses more gently, and maybe she's right. She pays the bills and who am I to argue. She makes me ride girls anytime they are available, but we don't have any local girls good enough to ride this horse."

"You don't happen to remember the date of this race do you?"

"It was about the middle of October last year."

One of the owners was pretty drunk by this time and spilled his drink all over the table. While the waitress was cleaning up, we all decided that we had all the fun we could handle for one day. The auction had one more day to run, and no one looked forward to being hung over. As soon as I got in my truck, I tried to call Goodman, but he didn't answer his cell. I would talk to him tomorrow.

When I arrived at the barn the next morning, the boys weren't present. I guessed they had so much fun at the sale they went straight there this morning. It figures that the first time I have something for them, they wouldn't show up. I had told them that I was going to enter their horse this morning and expected them to be here with bells on.

Other than the fact the boys were missing, the morning went routinely. It was still a fairly easy day because we had several walkers yet. I didn't expect to get in the first time I entered the horse and wasn't going to stay for the draw. I cornered the agent and got an ironclad agreement for his rider, but you can't ever depend on that agreement. We were finished by nine o'clock, and I went over and entered their horse. I made ten in the race, and it was still early so it would probably overfill.

The first page of the condition book usually has a list of all the jockeys and their agents, but when I checked it, Jodi wasn't there. It was too early for the agents to be coming in so I asked one of the entry clerks for the name of Jodi's agent. He had to ask three or four different people before someone gave him the answer. His name is John Miller. I now had enough information to allow Goodman to start checking him out.

I arrived at the sale about ten and noticed the parking lot was not nearly as full as yesterday. I parked and walked straight to the tent looking for Goodman. He was standing at the back talking to a bloodstock agent I knew to be a little shady. I knew he wasn't going to get sucked into buying another horse so I didn't interrupt their conversation. It would keep the salesman from working on someone that he might be able to scam.

I went out front away from people and called Pomona to see how my horses had shipped. He had the same opinion of the filly I did. He couldn't believe they were racing her when she was only about half broke. He had her shod and the farrier told him it would take three or four times to get her feet right. He asked if I was in a rush, and I told him to take all of the time he needed. He indicated that he didn't even want to send her to the track until her feet had grown out some and he had time to teach her to handle better. I agreed with his assessment and felt he was doing the right thing.

The colt was a different matter and he was going to start galloping tomorrow. He had just walked today because of the stress and activity of the sale, but he was ready to train. He had gone over him carefully and couldn't find anything wrong with him. I relayed the scuttlebutt about the knee surgery two years ago, and he promised to monitor him with that in mind. It sounded good so far, and I hung up and went back inside.

Goodman was still involved in his conversation, but I could see that he was tiring of the game. He was casting around for an escape route, and I thought I might as well give him one. I walked over and put my arm around the shoulder of the agent and said, "You're wasting your time with this one. I already got him involved for his whole bank roll. He might not recover for a year or two."

He laughed as if I had made a good joke, but it was only another five minutes before he excused himself to go and make a phone call. Goodman thanked me and admitted he didn't know how to break the conversations off after he got them started.

"You are a new face and everyone will be testing the water to see if you are a prospective customer. Don't worry about it."

"Did you enter the horse this morning?"

"Yeah, but the draw isn't over yet, so I don't know if we got in. I've got something to talk to you about. Let's find a little privacy."

We walked outside and he said, "I am parked in the second row. Let's go sit in the car. I got here early today."

As we walked to the car, I asked, "St. Germaine isn't with you today?"

"He'll be here a little later. He had to drive to the office in L A to pick up a packet of stuff they sent us from D. C. It's a terrible drive and he wanted to flip me to see who made it, but I told him I had to wait for you because you had some information for me."

"How did you know that?"

"I saw that you called me at nine o'clock last night so I guessed you may have found something in the printouts."

We reached the car and settled in before I started. "I may have found something, but it wasn't in the printouts. There is a rider named Jodi Breaux who is married to her agent. His name is John Miller, and he fits the profile of an aloof loner. No one knows anything about him, and he is near invisible. He was in the Ft. Worth-Dallas area of Texas about the middle of October, and I would suggest you check for a hit there during that time. The thing that makes him a person of interest to me is he was spotted in a shoe store buying a dozen pairs of tennis shoes. They don't have any kids so that seems really odd to me."

"Do you know this guy?"

"I never met him in my life and so far have found only one person who has. That person saw him buying the shoes. It appears that he does most of his business by telephone and tries to discourage business rather than look for it."

He sat thinking about what I had told him for a few minutes and finally said, "It sounds promising. I need to make some phone calls and I'll be in shortly."

Since I was being dismissed, I went back into the pavilion and bought a soda at the bar. I hung around for about an hour before I decided he wasn't coming back for awhile and walked down to the barns. I wasn't interested in anything else in the sale and just loafed around talking to a few people I knew but mostly just hanging out.

I ran into Mandy and she told me she would be finished by one o'clock and would meet me in the pavilion. I went back into the sale and when Goodman still wasn't there walked out to check his car. I t was gone and I had to believe that something had turned up to make them think this could be the guy.

Mandy appeared promptly at one o'clock, and since the boys still hadn't come back, we left. We stopped for lunch near the marina and when we reached the harbor red flags were flying at the entrance. When I explained that meant storm warnings, she suggested we not take the boat out. She was perfectly happy to spend the afternoon relaxing on the boat.

Late in the afternoon we walked across the street to one of the steak houses and had dinner and a couple of drinks. Mandy had followed me in her car so we didn't have to go back to the sale to pick it up. She said she didn't have to be home until the next day, and we spent the night on the boat.

I had to be at the track early so I showed her how to set the lock so that it clicked on when she pulled the hatch shut. I cautioned her to be sure she hadn't forgotten anything before she closed it and told her to stay as long as she wanted.

On the way to the track, I thought about how strange this was. I didn't know where she lived or where she worked, and didn't even have her phone number. She obviously wasn't just a horse groom since she was driving a little Mercedes convertible, and they weren't cheap. This was the first time I had even seen her car. I liked her and was comfortable with her and found the whole experience pleasant.

I stopped at the stable gate and picked up an overnight to see if my horse got in. He was in and had drawn the two hole.

You are never happy about your post position. With an older horse, you want inside spots and always seemed to draw outside; but with a first-time starter, you would prefer to be outside so he doesn't get caught in traffic and get in trouble. Here I was inside and grumbling when I should be happy that he got in at all.

I walked into the barn expecting the boys to be there, but they weren't. My assistant said he hadn't seen them for three days. I was only asking about this morning since I already knew they hadn't been here the two days prior, but I let it slide.

"If they come by, tell them their horse is in the second race tomorrow."

I had intended to enter three horses today, but when I checked the extras on the overnight there were two more races that I had horses for. I didn't want to run five horses in one day, but it would be unusual for all five races to go. I was glad that I had struck out at the entry box the other day and didn't have anything in today. Because of the auction and the trip to the boat with Mandy, I had made none of my phone calls this week. I would need to spend the afternoon making my calls. If I forget to call them, they start calling me, and it never fails that they call when it is most inconvenient.

We started to send the horses to the track, and I went to the grandstand. For some reason there seemed to be a much larger crowd of rail birds than normal. I couldn't imagine why until about eight o'clock when they started announcing some of the super stars as workers. I remembered that one of the big handicaps was this weekend, and they must have advertised that these horses were going to work today to create interest in the race. It must have been a good idea because there was a large crowd and it was still growing.

When my last horse left the track, I went back to the barn, but still no word from the boys. I did my paperwork and went over to enter my horses. The racing office was busy, and I had to wait for half an hour to make my entries. They ended up using all three of the regular races and one of the extras, and I got in with all four of my entries. It was going to be a tough afternoon on race day. The only problem I was going to have was one of the grooms had two of his horses in back to back and would need help. Grooms always whine when they have to help another groom run one of his horses, but sometimes it can't be helped.

On the way back to the barn I went by the kitchen on the chance the boys might be there, but they weren't. I gathered up my stuff, locked the office, and went home. I was so sure we had found our man I didn't even consider looking at the printouts. I had lunch and started on my calls.

Because my calls were a day or two late, everyone seemed grouchy and the calls went slower than was necessary. I had to talk each owner out of their bad mood and was in a bad mood myself by the time I finished. The owner I think is about to leave me was very distant and didn't express any interest as I gave him the races I thought we should enter. I had just finished my last call when the phone rang.

I snatched it up and said, "What?"

There was a long pause before Goodman said, "Don't bite my head off. I've been trying to call you for an hour. Who in the world have you been talking to?"

"Don't mind me. This was my day for calling all my owners, and it always leaves me thinking I'm in the wrong business. What's up?"

"Have you got time for me to stop by? We need to talk about a few things."

"Where are you?"

"I am parked in front of your apartment."

"How did you know where I live?"

"Give me a break. Have you forgotten I work for the FBI?"

"Have you been parked there for the hour you've been trying to call me?"

"Actually more like two hours. You have been a busy guy."

"Yeah, come on in."

I waited for him at the open door and motioned him in. He was carrying a zippered notebook and dressed in slacks and a polo shirt. I thought that he had started to like that mode of dress. He declined my offer of a beer and took a seat on the couch.

"I have a lot to go over with you. I normally wouldn't give a civilian all of the information I'm going to relate, but I can't take a chance you might step in a bear trap because you didn't know something important. And, after all, you found this guy for us.

"Your John Miller turns out to be Jon Molenaar. Oddly enough Molenaar is Miller in Dutch."

"Dutch? Isn't that interesting?"

"It gets a lot more interesting. Jon Molenaar served six years in the Dutch Special Forces. He dropped out of sight for several years after his discharge, and we are still trying to find where he went. He married Jodi Breaux twelve years ago and moved to the U S with a green card. That's just for starters.

"St. Germaine remembered the name Molenaar on the passenger list from the LAX thing. It turns out that Anders Molenaar was the private detective that was on that flight. It also turns out that Anders is Jon's older brother.

"Now for the interesting part. Anders was head of security for our Dutch bank of interest for twelve years before he came to the U.S. on a work visa. I don't know what head of security does for a bank, but his salary was indecently large.

"He now runs a company called the Triple M Detective Agency. We don't know yet who the third M is, but we're searching for him.

"This morning we sent one of our people, who is actually going through a divorce, to the agency on the pretense of having them dig dirt on her husband. On the outside the building is an ordinary, unpretentious, stucco building with no windows. It has a small brass plaque beside the door with the name on it but no other signs. When she entered, however, it was something completely different. It was built around a court yard and was all steel and glass. She reported that it was beautifully designed, and furnished with expensive modern furniture.

The receptionist directed her to a small office off of the entry, and a young well-dressed man proceeded to blow her off by telling her they don't do that kind of work. When she pretended to become agitated by his refusal to help her, he patiently explained they only handle industrial cases: Things like looking for company embezzlers, looking for industrial spies, proving patent infringements, and so forth. She said he was very polite but ushered her firmly out of the building.

The paper pushers are having trouble finding financials on Triple M but they will dig them out. You can bet on that. The difficulty they are having getting information makes it appear that it may actually be a foreign-owned company. They are trying to be extra careful in case the owner turns out to be our Dutch bank. They don't want to alert them to the fact an investigation is going on.

Another point of interest is the president of a fairly large chain of banks in Arkansas and Oklahoma was found in a high rise Dallas apartment building with a matched pair of twenty two slugs in his head. He was found on the twenty-fourth of October but had been dead for a week or more. It was his apartment, but he wasn't found earlier because he was not supposed to be there. He was thought to be visiting bank branches, and we don't know what lured him home.

This Jon guy is so slippery we don't even know where he lives. The address on his licenses application turned out to be a Chinese restaurant. He listed his mailing address as a PO Box, which was rented with cash and no one has been seen picking up mail from it. Her application has the same addresses but that doesn't mean she is involved. The TRPB looked at the applications and reported that the same person filled out both applications. The signature on hers was even suspect. She may have never even seen the application. Another interesting point is the stable where the two murdered grooms worked has ridden Jodi Breaux several times. We hadn't included the jockeys in our search when we checked out the connections of the stable. It's reasonable to assume that one or both would have at least seen him, thus constituting a threat."

I interrupted him to say, "I think I should have a picture of these two guys. If I run into either one of them, I would like to know who they are. Can you do that for me?"

"Sure. I'll bring them to the track in the morning. I think it's a good idea."

"Everyone at the office is really enthused about these guys. They are confident we have found our assassin. St. Germaine and I have been elevated to the status of genius for ferreting them out. I have been very careful to exclude your name from every report. I don't know how well these people are connected, and a lot of eyes may look at these reports before it's all over. I don't want you to be looking over your shoulder for the rest of your life."

"That suits me fine. I would be happy if my name was never mentioned to anyone. How are you going to handle this from here?"

"By tomorrow we'll have this guy covered like a blanket. A team of experienced watchers will arrive sometime tonight, and from then on we'll know when he brushes his teeth. They will have another team on Anders, but they didn't have one assembled yet so that may take a few days."

"I am amazed that someone in the horse business is actually doing these things. I was sure you guys were on a wild goose chase and it blows my mind."

"I knew you didn't have much confidence in our search and without your help we probably would have never found him. We were looking at the wrong people and would have never turned him up. Somehow we'll show our appreciation, but we're a long way from finished. We have to prove a case against both of them, and considering their track record, that could be a tough nut to crack."

Then he said, "To change the subject, how's our horse going to run tomorrow?"

"That's like sitting in a bar and betting on whether the next girl that walks in will be ugly or pretty. There is absolutely no way to predict how a first time starter is going to react and what kind of race he will run. I'll be happy if he learns something and doesn't hurt himself. Anything beyond that is a bonus."

As he started putting his paperwork back in his notebook, he said, "I understand, and we are not expecting anything out of the ordinary. We are excited about him racing, but it is just a side game for us. We aren't going to give you a bad time if it doesn't work out. I'll see you tomorrow."

After he left I opened a beer and sat thinking about the things he had just told me. I was relieved that it hadn't turned out to be someone I knew. It would have been unsettling to find that a person I interacted with on a daily basis killed people in his spare time.

I came to the barn in the morning with a good attitude. I could stop looking at all of my friends and wondering if they were leading a secret life. I didn't have to concentrate on anything but business—and it was a relief. The day was going to be easy compared to tomorrow when I had four horses in, and I took the time to enjoy my new found freedom.

I only had a pair to work and the rest were galloping. I didn't have any walking today and everyone went to the track except the colt that was racing. My crew didn't see it as an easy day with all of the horses going to the track, but I did. I was just leaving to go to the grand stand when Goodman came in. He handed me a manila envelope, and I peeked inside to see it contained pictures. I locked it in my desk drawer and went on up to watch my horses.

The morning went smooth with one exception. One of my horses was just coming on the track when a horse in front of him wheeled and dumped his rider. The outrider spurred his horse and made a run at the rider-less horse, trying to catch him before he bolted and ran away. A loose horse on the track is one of the most dangerous things that can happen. My horse propped, causing the rider to come off; but she is an excellent rider and she didn't fall, but rather just slid off holding the reins and landing on her feet. She managed to hold the reins until the horse settled down, preventing two loose horses on the track. I would be sure to give her an attagirl when I went back to the barn.

After I finished my paperwork, I went to the kitchen for lunch and was glad to find the boys weren't there. I hadn't discussed it with them, but I hoped they wouldn't be asking questions among the horsemen about Jon Miller. When I was twenty I thought I was bullet proof, but I have outgrown that kind of thinking. The last thing I wanted now was someone thinking I should be dead.

We were in an early race and I was glad of that. When you're just running one horse and he is in a late race, it makes for a long, boring day. I had two or three forms that I hadn't read yet, and that should be just about the right amount for the time I had to kill.

The boys walked in about an hour before race time, and I could see they were excited. I explained how it would play out before the race. They couldn't go with me to the receiving barn, but they could come into the saddling paddock. They have a place for owners to watch the race if they don't have seats up in the grandstand. If we hit the board, I would have to take the horse to the test barn and it would be quite a while before we got back to the barn. A lot of tracks around the country only test the winner, but here they test every horse that hits the board and the favorite if he didn't hit the board.

They called our race up and we all walked over together. We went into the receiving barn and the boys went on to the saddling paddock. Here they have a prerace vet check and a vet in the receiving barn who looks them over again. They also have a track farrier, who checks the shoes on every horse. The only thing good about it is if a horse has loosened a shoe or bent one, the farrier is right there to make repairs. This was a lot of new action for a first time starter. He was in a barn with twelve horses walking around and two dozen people moving among them, and sometimes they could get stirred up; but the colt took it in stride. He looked at things, but he didn't get flighty.

We all walked to the saddling paddock in the order of our post position. I could hear a colt behind us raising hell, and I was glad we didn't draw in next to him. I didn't need the aggravation of an excited colt next to one I was trying to keep calm. We went into the stall to saddle, and as always a crowd had gathered at the rail to watch. They do this with the hope that a horse is going to give them some sign that he is going to be the winner. My colt was watching the people very intently, but he didn't find any danger there and stayed calm. Of course, as a first timer, he had no idea what was in store for him. A colt that is calm the first time can become hell on wheels the second time when he knows what's coming.

As we went through the tunnel to the track I was thinking the next test was going to be how he handled being led by the pony boy. I didn't know if he has ever been hooked up with a pony in his life. A lot of trainers pony their horses instead of galloping them quite a bit, but I never do. I have seen more horses injured while being led by a pony than get hurt galloping.

When we came out of the tunnel and he saw the cast of thousands, his ears went straight up and started rotating like a radar receiver, but he didn't panic. He just watched and listened. I held my breath when the groom handed him off to the pony boy, but it went reasonably well. He walked sideways for a minute trying to stay away from the pony, but as soon as he realized that the rider on the pony had his lead rope and he really couldn't stay away from him, he settled down and fell in step.

So far so good, and we would know in about ten minutes if we had a racehorse or not. Once the gate opened it was up to him to prove to me that he wanted to run. Some horses love it and some hate it. Very seldom does a horse that hates racing ever win races, so you hope for one that thinks it's fun. They are the ones who do well.

He was having trouble galloping alongside the pony in the warm up, and the rider had the pony boy cut him loose. He picked him back up when they started to the gate. Another reason you don't like and inside post for first timers is that at most tracks they must stand in the gate longer while the other horses are loaded. At least here they loaded from inside and from the middle at the same time so it only took half as long.

When the gate opened, every horse in the field tried to change lanes. They were bouncing around like ping pong balls. This can happen in any age race, but it happen a lot more often in maiden races. My colt took two pretty good shots but he didn't stop running, and I had to think I had a runner—if he had the talent. You can't teach a horse to have heart. He does or he doesn't, and if he doesn't he will quit you every time the going gets tough. It was a six furlong race, and they only had to negotiate one turn. We were laying about the middle of the pack as they entered the turn, and he was getting a lot of dirt in his face, which is another first you worry about. He held his ground through the turn, and as they straightened out in the stretch, he started to make a little move. He was running about sixth or seventh when they came out of the turn and moved up to be third at the wire. To make it even better, he was a good third and only beat by about three lengths for the whole thing. I was well satisfied and hoped I could make the boys understand he had run a very good race.

I walked out on the track to meet the horse as they came back to be unsaddled. As the rider took his equipment off, I said, "Everything go OK? How did he feel?"

"I got knocked around pretty good at the start, but he handled it OK. It took away any chance we had to win, but he tried. He's going to be a good one, boss. I would like to ride him back."

Coming from a rider that didn't get many mounts, a request to ride the horse back would just be automatic, but this rider had all the business he needed so it meant he liked him. I was pleased about that and assured him he had the call.

I went over to the test barn and waited while they gave the horse a bath and cooled him out. After they collected the urine and blood samples, I signed the voucher and followed him back to the barn. It had taken about an hour and I wasn't sure the boys would still be there but they were.

They were still excited and both were waiting to see what I had to say. As usual Goodman did the talking. "I thought for a minute we were going to win it. He was really coming at the end. What did you think?"

"I think he ran a big race and is going to be a winner soon. He got a lot of dirt in his face and kept running. That's a good sign. A lot of colts give it up the first time they get dirt in their face. The rider liked him and wants to ride him the next time he runs. I think he's going to be OK."

"I can see how people get hooked on this. It is like owning a sports team. I don't think you would have any more fun watching your football team play than we had watching our horse run."

"It's sort of the same thing. You tense every muscle in your body trying to help you horse go faster."

"I'm glad you said that because I thought I was the only one. I think I'm going to be sore tomorrow. I may have strained something."

We all laughed and I said, "He appears to have come out of the race good, but I will know better in the morning. Injuries sometimes don't show up for a day or two."

"We would like to buy your dinner if you have the time," Goodman said. "Although I have to admit, we are on an expense account, and it will actually be Uncle Sam buying dinner."

"Well, in that case I accept. I've never gotten anything except the shaft from Uncle Sam before."

I locked the office and we drove up the street to a steak house. This would fill up with race goers after the races, but it was near empty this early. We got comfortable, and ordered a round of drinks before we had dinner.

When the drinks were delivered, Goodman said, "I think we should make a toast to our first race."

I held up my glass and said, "Here's to fast horses and those who love them." We clinked glasses and took a long drink.

They were still on a high from watching their horse in his first race, and they replayed the race a dozen times for me. Of course they didn't see the race the same way I did, but I didn't pour water on their enthusiasm. The horse had run a good race, but in their eyes he had nearly been the winner. He actually had never threatened the winner, but I didn't bother to point that out. I was satisfied with his performance and was content to let them believe he had run a better race than he really had. They were a little disappointed when I told them I didn't plan to run him back for two or three weeks. New owners never have a concept of how much recovery time a horse needs after a race.

We had finished our meal and ordered another round of drinks before they ran out of race talk and I asked, "Any news on Jon?"

Goodman gave his reply as if he was reading from a script. "No. But we don't expect any until he has another contract to perform. We have him under twenty-four hour surveillance. He almost never leaves his apartment so there isn't anything to report."

"How did you find where he lives?"

"The crew had to follow his wife home from the track."

"Do you have his phone tapped?"

"There are a couple of problems with that. First of all, we really don't have any evidence that is solid enough to ask a judge for a wiretap. And secondly, we don't think we should let people outside of our crew know we are watching him. But we did catch a break. He doesn't have a land line and since his cell phone is on the air waves, we are not breaking the law by listening. The problem with that is we can't use anything we get from it in his prosecution. We weren't smart enough to foresee that some of his conversations would be in Dutch, and we had to send the tapes to the home office to be interpreted. We are waiting on transcripts of three separate calls."

"Have you got the brother covered yet?"

"Our second crew of watchers arrived yesterday. As of today he is covered, but we have a problem with his phones. He has a dozen land lines, and we are not allowed to listen without having a court order. Plus, the calls that we would be most interested in are going to be coming from outside the U.S., which makes it a very murky situation. The FBI is not supposed to get involved outside the U.S. We are debating whether we should turn that part of our investigation over to Homeland Security. They have a lot more leeway than we do, but in the past they have jerked us around by not releasing all of their information to us. We don't know if seeing part of the data rather than none outweighs the danger of them blowing our gig out of the water by picking them up on some silly charge like money laundering."

The restaurant was starting to fill up and we decided to call it a day. I left them in the parking lot and went home. Tomorrow was a busy day and I didn't stay up very late.

On the drive to the track I was going over the coming day. I had four horses in, but I was giving the most thought to another horse in one of my races that I was thinking of claiming. In fact, he would probably go off as the favorite today. I had run against him three times and had a chance to get a good look at him. The only thing that was making me indecisive about taking him was a horse in tomorrow that I liked even more, and I only had one stall available. If I took this horse today, I couldn't take the one tomorrow. There might be multiple claims on both horses, and if I didn't get lucky, I wouldn't get either one. I also had the two at Pomona that I would need stalls for at some point.

The boys didn't put in an appearance and I was glad. I had a lot going on today, and I needed to pay attention to a lot of details. I had finished timing a pair of workers and was jotting in my notebook when my cell phone rang. It was the owner I suspected was shopping for a new trainer calling to tell me he had found one, and they would be picking up his horses this afternoon. I closed the call as pleasantly as I could and told him I would mail his final bill tomorrow.

Oddly I felt a sense of relief and didn't mind in the least losing him as a client. He was not my kind of a person, and it was always an effort to be civil to him. He had been an owner for years and still didn't understand the business. The fact that I would have stalls available made it a win for me.

None of his horses had come to the track yet today. I called my assistant and told him not to send them to the track and to get them ready to ship out. I would take no chances they might sustain an injury after he told me he was moving. He is the kind of guy who would accuse me of doing it deliberately.

The rest of the morning went smoothly and I stopped at the racing office on the way back to the barn to make an entry. When I reached the barn, there was still no sign of the boys, and I had to assume they were busy with their suspect. I was finishing my paperwork when four grooms came to pick up the horses. They were all ready to go with shipping wraps on because I didn't know if he was sending a van for them or not. Since they were just going a few barns away, they were going to lead them over.

The activity at the barn was kind of hectic because of so many in today. The vet was there treating a horse with bleeder medication and the farrier was there to shoe three horses that were running later in the week. I don't normally shoe a horse the day he is in. I prefer to put on the shoes a day or two before in case a nail gets driven to close to the quick. If this happens they sometimes don't show soreness until the next day and I have time to get it corrected. I will only shoe a horse the day he is racing when it requires a change of shoes because the track comes up muddy.

After I was sure everything was going according to plan, I went back to the racing office for the draw. It was the usual bunch of agents and one or two trainers in attendance. My horse drew in, and I was walking out the door as they were drawing the next race. The first horse out of the box had Jodi Breaux named as the rider, and I stopped to see if her agent was there. He wasn't and there was no controversy over her being named on. The draw went on in a normal manner, and I went back to the barn.

The first of my horses running today was in the second race so I didn't have to be in jail too long. By the time I ate lunch at the kitchen, it was nearly time to go. The only place I would have trouble was the back to back races I had in the fifth and sixth. My assistant would take the horse in the sixth to the receiving barn and on to the paddock. If the horse in the fifth hit the board, I would meet him in the saddling paddock and saddle the horse while he went to the test barn to sign off on the test.

I had mixed emotions about this race. The horse was running one notch above where he should be in claiming price. There were three or four horses that ran at this level, that I couldn't outrun and I had been trying to talk the owner into dropping him a notch, but so far hadn't succeeded. They had enough horses to split this race, and I had gotten really lucky at the draw. All of the horses that I knew I couldn't outrun had drawn in the second half, which was the third race on the card. The problem was going to be convincing the owner that we were running this horse to high if he won today. Of course I hoped he won, but I might never be able to win at this level again, and I would be stuck here for several wasted races if he did.

The owner and his wife came down to the saddling paddock and stood in the parade ring before going back to their box for the race. I had told him how lucky we had been at the draw when I called to let him know about the race, but owners only hear what they want to hear. I could write this horse off for awhile if he won today.

The race went off clean, and the horse had as good of a trip as he could ever have and just got up at the end to win by a head. The owner and his wife were elated in the winner's circle, and I could see trouble on the horizon. If they asked me to move him up another step in claiming, we were going to have real problems.

After the pictures and the hand shaking and back slapping was over, they went off to celebrate. They asked me to go to dinner with them, but I explained I had a full day and would be exhausted at the end. I tried to not go out with my owners any more than I had to. We are business associates and not social friends. The more they think of you as a friend the more they expect from you and it never ends well. I try to keep socializing to a minimum.

As I came out of the winner's circle, a gentleman was waiting for me that I recognized as an owner of a good friend of mine. I had seen him around a lot and had even had lunch in the kitchen with him and my friend once.

He put out his hand and said, "I don't know if you remember me or not. My name is Ralph Kinder, and I would like to talk to you a minute if you have the time."

I shook his hand and said, "Sure, I remember you. You're one of Bob Ross's owners. Let's walk over in the shade."

We found a spot with a little space and I said, "What can I do for you?"

"I was wondering if you have room for a couple of horses."

I didn't like the sound of that. Bob was a good friend and I didn't want him to think I had solicited one of his clients. "Are you and Bob having trouble?"

"No, it's nothing like that. Bob is shipping to Florida next week and I don't want to send my horses with him. I like to go to the races and watch them run and it loses its appeal for me when I have to watch them on T V."

"I'll have to talk to Bob first. I can't take them if it's going to cause hard feelings between us. He's a good friend of mine."

"I'm sure there won't be any hard feelings. He understands my situation and, in fact, suggested I come to you."

I gave him my training rates and left with the understanding that I would talk to Bob in the morning, and if Bob was okay with it I would take his horses.

The horse I wanted to claim was in the fourth race, and I went to the racing office to drop my claim. I had until fifteen minutes before the race to drop it, but since I had a horse in the fifth I would be in the receiving barn at that time. I told the claims clerk that one of my people would be there to represent me.

I went to the test barn to check on my horse and got there just in time. They were finished with him and I had to sign off on the test samples.

I went back to the barn and only had a few minutes to wait before they called us over for the next race. I followed the horse to the receiving barn and was starting to think that I needed one more assistant trainer. I didn't have this much activity every day, but I could maybe squeeze in a little time off if I had another assistant.

Everything was good in the receiving barn, but when we arrived in the saddling paddock, the horse in the slot next to us pitched a bitch. He dragged his handler all over the place and finally ended up rearing over backwards. They finally got him saddled, and I was surprised the paddock judge hadn't scratched him because of the flip. He was still acting up in the parade ring, and I kept my horse well away from him. I was concerned about the break because he was coming out of the gate next to my horse.

We made it to the track without a mishap, but during the warm up the wild child threw his rider and ran off. It took the outriders a while to catch him, and the track vet scratched him. I was relieved that he wouldn't be breaking next to me. This was a race for older horses, and the only excuse for that kind of behavior was that the horse was just sour. He was over-raced or in pain but for whatever reason he didn't want to do it anymore.

By the time they got the horse off the track, we had to go straight to the gate so no one had time for a proper warm up. The horses all went in quietly and the race got underway with no other problems. I didn't like my chances and was happy with a solid third. He ran a decent race and was only beaten about two lengths.

As we were waiting for the horses to come back, my groom came to tell there had been three claims on the horse in the fourth, and we had lost the shake. That's the way it goes and there is always tomorrow. I hoped I would have better luck tomorrow because I really liked the horse.

When we unsaddled and the groom started for the test barn with the horse, I went to the saddling paddock to do the next race. I told the assistant that if we made the test barn with this one, to stay at the test barn and sign off on both horses since the one from the last race would probably not be finished yet. I would go back to the barn to bring the last horse over. He wasn't in until the eighth race and I would have plenty of time.

I had a shot at winning this race and got lucky again. The horse that I was most worried about got boxed in on the rail coming down the stretch and didn't get clear in time to make a run at the win. That is the problem with late running closers. If they get a bad trip, they lose their chance of winning. I won by a clear three lengths and hoped the easy win wouldn't make his owner decide we were running him too cheap. We were running him right where he should be, and I wanted him to stay at that level.

The owners were there with several friends, and we had a dozen people in the win picture. They had all imbibed a little bit, and it got a little loud and rowdy. The horse acted up some and one of the guys nearly got knocked down. That settled them down somewhat, and they were not as active but just as loud. When the groom left with the horse for the test barn, I went back to the barn.

The horse for my last race of the day was not very high on my list. He is what I class as a counterfeit. Some trainers call them morning glories. He has all of the speed you could ever ask for, but he won't give it to you in a race. Work him in the morning by himself and he will give you race winning times, but as soon as another horse looks him in the eye, he's done. He doesn't seem to be intimidated or afraid of the other horses; he just doesn't try to outrun them. He is happy to just gallop along with the pack. I have talked to several trainers that had such a horse in the past and none of them ever made him a winner. The only one I ever talked to who said he had a cure suggested something I couldn't do. He had started on the bush tracks of Louisiana and thought the only cure for that kind of horse was to plug him in, which means use an electric buzzer on the horse. Years ago you would see them around, and rumor had it that some riders would ride with them, but not anymore. The riders today are making so much money they would have to be crazy to jeopardize their careers for one horse or to win one race. In most cases the penalty these days for getting caught using a machine is a lifetime ban from racing. A rider who is making several hundred thousand dollars a year is not going to risk that to win an extra ten thousand on a race. It wouldn't make sense.

They called our race over and I followed the horse to the barn. I felt that I was just going through the motions with no hope of winning, and he didn't disappoint me. He galloped along from start to finish in the middle of the pack. The only decent thing about him was he didn't make me spend an hour in the test barn. I have suggested to the owner that he should find the horse a new home, but he wasn't ready to give up on him yet. He is a big good looking colt that at today's prices for high class jumping prospects is worth a lot more in the show ring than on the racetrack. He doesn't have a pimple on him, and I feel sure he would vet out sound. He refuses to run fast enough to hurt himself.

I went home tired but satisfied. Two wins and a third from four starts was a great day. I was a little disappointed about not getting my claim, but you can always buy a horse. All it takes is money.

The first thing I did in the morning was go over to talk to Bob Ross about his owner that wanted to give me his two horses. Bob was a great guy and when I was first starting out had given me a lot of help. He was a regular on the fair circuit during the summer. In the beginning when I had a horse that wasn't doing well at the tracks here, I would run a few races at the fairs. I would ship up and run and come home rather than stay on the circuit. He would always make sure I had a stall for my horse and helped me in every way he could. I would never forget the favors he did for me and had no intention of doing anything that might harm our friendship.

He was at the barn and when I asked about Ralph's horses, he was adamant that I take them. He was happy that I was getting them and asked if I could pick them up today. He not only had some owners that didn't plan to ship their horses with him but had several grooms that didn't want to go. Three of them hadn't shown up for work this morning, and he was going crazy trying to take care of his horses short-handed. I promised him I would pick them up right away and wished him luck in Florida.

On my way to the grandstand, I called my assistant and asked him to send two grooms over to get the horses. I could appreciate trying to run a barn short-handed. Racetrack grooms are notoriously unreliable and it is not uncommon for two or three of them to ship out for some faraway track with another outfit with no warning. The day after payday you always come to work in the morning hoping you still have a full crew.

Midway through the morning, I saw a kid that used to be my assistant coming up the steps to the grandstand. He had ambitions of becoming a trainer and had quit when he found a guy that was willing to give him four horses to train. I could have told him that he couldn't make it with four horses, but he didn't ask for my advice. He was a good assistant in that he would do anything you asked him to do. His shortcoming was he didn't do anything you didn't ask him to do. I hadn't seen him in over a year and guessed he had gone out of town with his horses to a smaller track.

As he walked up, I said, "Hi, Gene. How are you doing?"

He was a big boy well over six feet tall, and he sat down next to me and stretched his legs over the seat in front before he said, "Not worth a damn. I'm broke and looking for a job."

He hadn't specifically asked me for a job, but it was sort of implied. "I might work you in, but I have to talk to James, my assistant, first. He's doing a good job and I don't want to lose him."

"At this point I would take anything. If nothing else let me walk a few hots for enough to eat on."

I gave him the three twenty dollar bills I had in my pocket and said, "I can't let you starve to death. I have a horse in the fourth race. I'll talk it over with James and let you know then."

He knew I didn't like to have conversations while I was watching my horses train and stood up to leave. "I'll catch you after the fourth. Thanks for the loan."

As I watched him go down the steps, I was trying to think of how I could use him. I had toyed with the idea of a second assistant but had never worked it out in my mind how I could make it worthwhile. It is hard enough to cope with the bickering and jealousy among the grooms. The last thing I need is two assistants fighting over who is in charge. I would talk it over with James and see what he thought.

I was walking down from the grandstand when my cell phone rang. It was my friend from Pomona, and he wanted to tell me about my horses. I sat down on the steps and listened.

"I worked your gelding this morning and he was impressive. He went five-eighths in fifty nine flat and didn't take a deep breath. He not only appears ready to run; I think he can. You might have scored with this one."

"That's great. How's the filly coming along?"

"She has gained about thirty pounds and is starting to play on the walker a little. Two more weeks of foot growth and I will re-shoe her, and if her feet are looking better, I may start sending her to the track. She is a work in progress and I don't think we should rush her."

"I agree completely and just asked out of curiosity. Give her as much time as you think she needs. Have you been taking the gelding through the gate? He hasn't started in so long they may ask me to get him a gate OK before they let him start."

"He goes through it every morning and has never blinked an eye at it. He'll be OK."

"So what do you think? Should I bring him over and give him a try?"

"I think so. He has been training somewhere and I don't know why they sold him."

"Will you be around the barn at feeding time tonight?"

"It doesn't make any difference what time you come. I'm staying in my trailer in the trailer park. If I'm not at the barn, just knock on the door."

"OK, I'll pick him up sometime this afternoon. I have a horse in the fourth and one I'm going to try to claim in the fifth, and I'll be over after that."

"Very good. I'll see you then."

When I got back to the barn, I called James in and asked him to sit down before I said, "What do you think about my hiring an assistant's assistant for you?"

He looked like he had swallowed a bug as he said, "What would he do?"

"That's what we need to talk about. I was thinking I would have him licensed as an assistant so when we need the extra coverage he would be qualified; but actually I would use him as a barn foreman. He could ride herd on the grooms and take care of the mechanics of operating the barn. That would free you up to be more involved in the training than you are now. I still want you to be in charge of everything pertaining to the horses themselves. I want you overseeing their medications, shoeing, and everything else you consider important. You would be the boss just as you are now, but you wouldn't have to take care of every little detail. You tell me how you think it should work."

"Is it someone I know?"

"I don't think you know him but you might. His name is Gene Smith. He worked for me before you came around. He is the kind of guy who will do everything you tell him to do but not one iota more. He is not much of an independent thinker but will take care of all of his duties. I think you two would get along well, and he is not the kind of guy who would backstab you trying to get your job."

"I'm not sure we need him, but if you want to try it, I guess it's OK with me."

"I'm going to the racing office to make an entry and you think it over while I'm gone. If you decide you don't like the idea, I'll forget about it. How did the two horses look that came over from Bob Ross?"

"They both look good. I gave them to Henry since he lost the four yesterday."

"Tell him I'm trying to claim one today, and I'm picking one up from Pomona this afternoon. He'll still have four to rub."

I went to the racing office and arrived just in time to find all of the agents pouring out of the door. When I asked what was going on, they told me we were going to have a foot race for five hundred dollars. The only thing making this interesting was that it was a fat man's race. The two agents that were going to race both weighed over three hundred pounds. I went in and made my entry, and went out to watch.

They had first intended to race on the track but decided it was too deep and soft. They settled on the apron and one of the other agents stepped off fifty yards. There was a lot of trash talk going on and even some betting among the agents. They had one agent stand as the starting pole and one stand as the finish, and another counted ready set go. They were pretty even for the first twenty five yards before one ran out of gas and gave it up. The last man standing slowed to not much more than a jog for the last ten yards, but he was the winner. When you are a gambler and have too much money, I guess you'll bet on anything.

When we went back inside, I was told that the race I had entered in was being called off, and they wanted to know if I wanted to move the horse to a different race. I didn't. With no point in hanging around, I picked up a claim slip and went back to the barn.

When I reached the barn, James came into the office and sat down. "I guess it wouldn't hurt to try it for awhile. You have to make it clear to the new guy that I am in charge. I don't want him arguing over everything I say, and if the guys think they can play one of us off against the other, the whole barn will fall apart."

"I agree that it would fall apart. I will make it very clear to him that you are and will always be the boss. I promise I want let that become a problem."

I went in the office and filled out the claim slip and gave it to James to drop for me. I was going to run the horse in the fourth and would be tied up. I said I would go with the horse to the test barn if we hit the board and he should wait around to see if we got the claim. He arranged for one of the grooms to meet him at the office to lead him back in case we did.

I had two hours to kill so I went to the kitchen for lunch. I was joined at my table by a trainer that I didn't particularly like, but what can you do. He is a habitual cry baby, and I had a half hour of listening to all of his woes. It was so boring I wanted to scream, and as soon as I was finished eating, I walked over to watch one of the card games.

I went back to the barn and when I sat down at my desk I had an eerie feeling that it wasn't normal. I am a person that keeps a messy desk, but it is a controlled mess and I know where everything is. It didn't feel right and I couldn't say why exactly. I called James in and asked if anyone had been in the office. He said no; he had been in the shed row the entire time I was gone to lunch and hadn't seen a soul. I unlocked the drawer that had the pictures of Jon and Anders, and they were still there. The feeling wouldn't go away, and I was spooked enough that I ran the pictures through my little paper shredder. I looked around the office to make sure there wasn't anything else I didn't want anyone to see. I was still trying to locate whatever it was that had bothered me when they called for us to come over for our race.

When the groom handed the horse to the pony boy, I turned around to find a spot to watch the race from and there was Gene. Once the horses go on the track, the apron fills up pretty fast and gets noisy. I took him back inside under the grandstand and it was a little quieter.

I told him what I needed and what the rules would be. "James is my assistant and will be the boss. I need you as a barn foreman, but I am going to have you licensed as an assistant so you can fill in when it's needed. If you can't get along with James, you will have to find another job. I won't put up with any squabbling between the two of you. The barn is running smooth now, and I need to keep it that way. If you can live with that, come to work in the morning."

He looked as if I had insulted him a little as he said, "That's fine with me. I'll be there in the morning. What's the pay for a barn foreman?"

"I'll start you at the same salary you made before, and we'll see how it goes."

They were putting the horses in the gate and I found a spot where I could see the race. He ran a decent race, but he was another one of those horses I would run a little bit cheaper if he belonged to me. He finished third, and I was satisfied that he had run as well as he could run. I followed him over to the test barn and watched while they gave him a bath.

When I got to the barn, I went out to the lot and hooked up my trailer. I drove over to Pomona to pick up the gelding I had bought at the auction. He was looking fit, and I liked him better than when I had seen him at the sale. We loaded him with no problem, and I took a look at the filly since I was there. He was right about her having gained weight and she acted as if she was feeling better also.

Before I left I asked, "How far from a race do you think the gelding is?"

"If he was mine, I would enter him tomorrow. He's as ready as he's ever going to be. What price are you thinking of starting him for?"

"I think about twelve five. That's a pretty soft bunch right now, and I think it's easier than the ten thousand level."

"I think you're right, and I also think you should make a little wager on him. Being off for two years, he may go off at fifty to one."

"Evidently you really think he is ready."

"This horse can run a little, and I wouldn't be surprised if he could win for twenty-five or thirty today."

"I'll look at my condition book when I get back to the barn and see what I can find for him. I'll call you when he's going to run." We shook hands and I went back to the track.

The groom had left, but he had his stall bedded and his water bucket and hay net hung, so I put him away and went into the office. I didn't want to leave until he had a few minutes to settle down in case he acted up in his new surroundings. He went straight to the hay net and acted like he had always lived there. I sat looking at my office still trying to figure out what had triggered my subconscious to suspect someone had searched it.

A note on my desk from James said, "Sorry boss, six claims and we got out shook again." Damn the bad luck. I really liked this horse for the price and had hoped to get him.

Nothing caught my attention that proved someone had been through my office, but I couldn't shake off the feeling. After I was sure the new horse was going to be all right, I went home.

I didn't feel like making my own dinner so I stopped and ate on the way home. I was still going over the office in my mind when I reached home and decided to get rid of everything there that connected me with the Bureau's case. I took every scrap of the printouts and everything I had written down to the alley and burned it in an empty trash can. I realized I was acting paranoid, but someone had searched my office. I didn't know yet how I knew, but I did.

I switched on the TV and sat down to watch a ball game. I must have dozed off, and when the phone rang, I jumped so hard I think I strained a muscle in my side. I picked it up and the voice on the other end was Goodman's.

"Hi Chance, it's Robert Goodman. How are you doing?"

"I'm about half way. What's up?"

"I just wanted to give you a heads up. One of the computer geeks at the Los Angeles office thinks someone has been into our computer. He says whoever did it is really, really, good. He thinks anyone that good is a big money earning professional and not some kid hacking for a lark. Our guy hasn't been able to see yet what he was pulling off, but he thinks it was dossiers on the staff. Our crew of watchers isn't attached to this office so they wouldn't be there, but William and I are. Nothing in the whole office has your name on it, but if he is tracking us, you may end up on his radar screen."

"It's funny you should call tonight. I think someone searched my office today."

A long pause ensued while he thought this over, and then he said, "That's not good. Do you own a gun?"

"All I have is a rifle, but it wouldn't do me any good anyway. You can't have a gun on the race track and the penalty is severe."

"Let me see what I can do. If I can get a federal gun permit issued, it will supersede state laws and allow you to carry it anywhere. In the meantime be careful and watchful at all times. You have a small advantage because you know who he is. It's not as bad as having a stranger walk up to you in a crowd and try to kill you."

"I'm confused about how he would even know you were looking at him already. I thought your watchers were better than that."

"I don't think he knows we are looking at him. I think this is coming back from the financial digging the paper pushers have been doing. This is above his capabilities, and he wouldn't be nosing around if he suspected we had an eye on him."

"If that's true why would he search my office?"

"That's a good question, and it worries the hell out of me. I'll discuss this with our people in the morning and let you know what we decide. I think I should stay away from the track for a few days, but I will talk to you sometime tomorrow."

After Goodman said goodnight and hung up, I switched off the TV and sat thinking about the whole affair. I couldn't understand how he had got on to me so quickly. It didn't make sense any way I looked at it. The only thing for sure was that I would be very cautious for the time being.

I took my rifle out of the closet and loaded it. It gave me a small sense of security, but the key word was small. I first stood it beside my bed and didn't like my chances of getting to it if he came sneaking in. I finally laid it on the offside of the bed with the barrel pointing toward the foot. It seemed like the place where I would have the best chance of getting to it in an emergency. I went to bed, but I lay awake a long time.

By the time I reached the barn in the morning, Gene and James were already acquainted. James was taking him down the shed row introducing him to the crew. It looked like it was going well so I didn't butt in. I went on into the office and made ready for my day.

The day was going to be typical with a couple to work and three or four to walk and the rest to gallop. I had one to run this afternoon, and unfortunately he was in the last race. He was a cheap horse that belonged to me, and I was thinking I might let James run him for me and go on home after training. I hadn't slept very well; I was tired, and the thought of sitting around all afternoon didn't appeal to me at all.

I went to the grandstand without too much enthusiasm and watched my horses. About halfway through the morning, my cell phone rang. I answered and Goodman said, "Is there anything in your apartment that connects you to us?"

"Just your names in my account book. Why?"

"Jon is at this minute in your apartment."

That stunned me for a minute before I asked, "Doesn't that give you a reason to arrest him?"

"Sure, but then he would know we are watching him. That's the last thing we should do. It is a minor charge that wouldn't cause him much of a problem, and he would be out in an hour. He would probably just disappear, and this would have all been for nothing. If you don't have anything there that puts you in jeopardy, we will let it slide as if it never happened."

"After I felt my office had been searched, I went home and burned everything. There's nothing left that would make him suspicious of me."

"That's great. It might even take you off his radar screen. I'll talk to you later." And with that he hung up.

I was glad I had put my rifle back in the closet this morning before I left. It would have looked funny lying on the bed loaded. My accelerated heart beat told me very plainly that I was scared of this guy, and it was an hour or so before I felt normal. It was hard to stay focused on business when you were thinking your life might be in danger. I even missed one of my workers and had to estimate the time for my journal.

My phone rang again, and since I never look at the number that's calling, I assumed it was Goodman again. I was surprised when it turned out to be James calling from the barn. He wanted to know what I wanted to do with the gelding I had brought over from Pomona. I hadn't put him on the training schedule yet, and since he was playing in his stall, he thought we should send him to the track. I agreed that if he was playing he should go to the track before he hurt himself. It was evident when he came on the track that he was feeling his oats. He didn't try to run away, but you could see he was feeling good and wanted to play around but was too well trained to do it. A twelve-five race was in the book tomorrow. I was going to talk to the starter, and if he had no objections, I would enter him.

By the time I came down from the grandstand, I had decided I was going to spend the night on the boat. I felt sure he wouldn't know about the boat, and I should be safe there for a day or two. It would also be much harder for anyone to approach me without warning because the boat would move if someone stepped aboard. I wish I had a rifle on the boat, but all I had there was a flare pistol. I had never fired it at anything, but it looked effective in the movies.

I had two entries to make, and since I wanted to catch the starter when he came to the racing office to post the works for the day, I went there first. I made my entries and hung around a half hour before the starter came in. I explained that the horse hadn't started for quite a while but had been training at Pomona and walking through the gate every day. He said he would give me one start, and if the horse acted up, he would put him on the starter's list and I would have to work him off of it. I thanked him and went back to the barn.

I talked to the exercise rider that had taken the new gelding to the track, and she gave good reports all around. She liked his way of going, he was traveling sound, and he seemed very fit. If he belonged to a client, I would have put a work or two on him myself before I entered him, but since he was mine, I skipped this step. I told James I had some business to take care of and he should run my horse in the last. I went over for the draw and left.

On my way to the boat, I stopped for a few groceries in case I ended up staying for more than one or two nights. I also wanted a chance to see if anyone was following me. It wouldn't do any good to hide on the boat if I led him right to it. When I left the store, I went down the side alley and drove around the block to see if anyone was looking confused about which way to go. I looked at the cars carefully, trying to implant them in my mind in case one of them was following me later. About half way to the boat, I pulled into a shopping center that had a large liquor store. I didn't want any booze, but I needed to see if another car also pulled into the lot. One did, but it pulled up beside me in front of the store and the driver was a little fat lady of about fifty. I sat there for five minutes without seeing anything out of the ordinary and drove on to the boat.

I unloaded my groceries and put them away before I went up into the cockpit. I opened a soda and sat on deck for two hours just watching people coming and going. It was a nice afternoon, and I felt very relaxed although I paid more attention to the people moving around than I usually would. When I came back down to the cabin, I dug out my flare pistol and loaded it. I put the pistol and two extra flares in the little niche beside my bunk. I was as ready as I could make myself, but I hoped this was needless preparation.

My phone rang, and when I answered Goodman said, "Everything OK with you?"

"Yeah, but I didn't go home. I'm on my boat at the marina."

"That's not a bad idea, but Jon is at home. We have him sewed up tight; he would have to turn into a bat to get out without us seeing him. The reason I'm calling is to let you know I have permission to issue you a federal gun permit. As soon as you can make it to the Los Angeles office for your pictures and fingerprints, we can issue it. Is tomorrow a good day?"

"Tomorrow would be very good. They didn't use the race I entered in, so I don't have anything running."

"How about I meet you in the Bureau office at one o'clock?"

"That's a good time. I'll be there."

He gave me the address and directions and hung up.

I had some trash to take to the dumpster and had waited until late because I wanted to be sure the gate was locked. Sometimes people that were taking things to and from their boat propped it open to make it easier. That locked gate wasn't going to be much of a deterrent to anyone who really wanted in, but every little bit helped. I would feel better with it locked.

The night was perfect for me. The water was smooth and there was no movement of the boat whatsoever. If the wind had been blowing and the boat moving around a lot, I would probably have been suicidal by morning. I slept without any interruptions and felt great in the morning. I ate breakfast on the way to the track and arrived a little early.

The day started with a bonus when the agent of the rider I wanted for the new gelding came by the barn just as I walked up. I got a firm commitment from him to ride the horse. An agent's firm commitment is not chiseled in stone, but this guy rides a lot of horses for me and shouldn't spin me in a cheap race.

I asked James how things were going between him and Gene, and he said everything was good. I thought that as soon as he saw how much work it was going to take off of him, he would like the new setup. Unless he had changed a lot, Gene was not the aggressive type that would try to undercut anyone. I thought it would work.

I had a normal schedule on tap for the day with six workers and six walkers. Everything else galloped and the morning went good. I had two other horses to enter besides my new gelding and stopped in the office to make my entries on the way to the barn. When I got back to the barn, Gene was explaining to James why he didn't like the job one of the grooms was doing. I listened to the last part of the conversation without getting into the discussion. I had reservations about this groom myself and was curious how James would handle it. The discussion ended with James saying he would have a talk with the groom, and if that didn't straighten him out, he would replace him. These old experienced grooms will push you to the limit, testing how much you will let them get away with, and this one hadn't been carrying his weight lately. James knew it and I knew it, but I couldn't blame James for not taking care of it when he had the responsibility of the whole operation on his shoulders. Having a barn foreman would put the spotlight on these guys and maybe improve the operation of the whole barn. One or two of them would probably quit and look for an easier job, but that couldn't be helped.

I did my paperwork and went back to the racing office for the draw. Fortunately I didn't fool around because they closed early and were starting the draw when I walked in. They used two of the races I had entered in, and one of them was the new horse. I got acceptable post positions in both races and didn't have a problem with my riders. I had told James I was going from the draw to an appointment and wouldn't be back to the barn.

On the way downtown, I kept a close eye on the traffic behind me. I thought I should be OK because no one would expect me to leave the track this early, but I didn't want anyone following me to the office of the FBI. I couldn't have deniability if someone followed me there.

I told the receptionist I was there to see Robert Goodman, and she called him on the phone. He came right out to meet me and took me down the hall to have my picture and my fingerprints done. The whole process didn't take more than fifteen minutes, and we went back to Goodman's office to wait for the permit. In the movies you always see an office with ten or twelve guys at their desks sharing one room. I was surprised to find the office Goodman took me to had just two desks with him and St. Germaine in it.

St. Germaine shook my hand and gave me a rare smile without saying anything. He sat back down at his desk and Goodman indicated a chair for me beside his desk.

When I was seated, he said, "It shouldn't take more than a half hour. Would you like a cup of coffee or a soda?"

"I'm OK. Anything new?"

"No, not really. Other than the trip to your apartment, he hasn't left his digs. We did get a handle on where he spent the eight years after his army discharge."

"I don't suppose he was sunbathing on the beach somewhere, was he?"

He smiled and said, "He was in the sun, but it wasn't on the beach. He was on the security force that patrols the diamond mines in South Africa. Do you know anything about what goes on there?"

"Not a lot, but I think they deal with those people pretty harshly."

"That's putting it mildly. They patrol a hundred-mile-wide strip around the diamond mines. They call it no man's land and they have one directive. Anyone caught in it dies. It is a brutal undertaking and the average time a soldier—if you want to call them that—serves on this force is less than two years. Anyone who served more than three or four years can be classed as a true sociopath. Our man spent eight years there. That speaks very loudly of a man who enjoys killing. It not only involves the killing of men but involves torture and brutality you can't imagine. If they catch them going in, the torture is to find out who else is involved, and if it is coming out it is to find out if they have hidden diamonds anywhere. If they are coming out, they cut them open front and back to make sure they haven't swallowed a diamond or stuck one up their ass. We have observed them from satellite surveillance doing this while the guy is still alive. Anyone who can take this duty for eight years is a sick son of a bitch."

He stopped to see if I was getting the full picture before he continued, "Because Jon is considered so dangerous is the reason we are giving you a gun permit. If he approaches you in any private setting such as your apartment or your boat, don't wait to see what might be on his mind, just blow his head off. I promise you there won't be any repercussions. Am I clear on this? This guy is not normal in any way."

"I'm clear enough to know you are scaring me to death."

"I'm trying to. I need to be sure if he ever confronts you there is no hesitation on your part. I would hate to think you died because I hadn't convinced you of the danger this guy presents. He may be the most dangerous person you have ever encountered, and I have to be sure you understand that."

We were interrupted by a knock on the door, and a young lady entered and handed Goodman an envelope. He thanked her and opened the envelope and handed me my gun permit, saying, "It's time to go buy you a gun. Have you given any thought to what you should get?"

"Not really. What do you suggest?"

"I would suggest a Smith & Wesson thirty-eight police special. Under the circumstances I think it would be the most practical. It is small enough to carry with ease and with uses special defense bullets powerful enough to get the job done. An automatic can be a little complicated if you are not accustomed to handling them whereas the police special is a revolver so you just point and pull the trigger. It only holds six shots, but in the event you have to use it, you are only going to get one shot so that's not important. It's the gun a lot of us carry as a backup."

"What do you mean by special defense bullets?"

"I'm sure you have heard of hollow point bullets. They are designed to spread on impact, giving a much larger jolt. They manufacture a bullet now that is much better than a hollow point. It is considered to be for defense only and almost explodes on impact. If you shoot a man anywhere on his torso he is going to die. They aren't accurate beyond about twenty-five feet, but you aren't going to have a long range gun battle. I will give you a box of the brand we use."

"Where do you suggest I buy a gun?"

"I am going to take you to a gun shop where we all shop. I am hopping he will think you are one of us and not impose the waiting period on you. We'll go whenever you're ready."

"I'm as ready as I'll ever be."

We went to the parking garage and took his car, and on the way over he said, I'll pick out the gun and holster and you keep browsing around. When he's ready to do the paper work, I'll ask you to toss your permit to me. Hand it to me and keep browsing like it's no big deal. With a little luck, he'll write it up from your permit and not ask for your badge."

We went into the store, and it had everything I could imagine. There was no problem with finding something to browse through. You could spend all day in here and not see it all. The plan worked to perfection, and I paid him in hundred dollar bills, and we walked out with the gun in a shopping bag.

When we reached the parking garage, Goodman opened his trunk and handed me a box of shells. "Load it now and carry it on you at all times until this is over. If you should run afoul of track security or even the police, give them my number and I'll take care of it. The federal permit should tell either one of those groups that you're above their pay grade, and they should leave you alone. If they don't know that, just call me."

"Thanks for everything. I'm praying I don't ever need the gun, but I do feel better having it."

"I hope you don't need it, but don't hesitate if he comes after you. This holster clips on your belt, and I suggest you clip it in the small of your back and wear your shirt out to cover it. You'll get used to it in a day or so."

We shook hands and I went back to my pick up. I did feel much better having the gun, and I hoped that if the situation arose, I wouldn't be afraid to use it. I had no reason to go back to the barn, and since I was already half way to the boat, I went there. The first thing I did was unload the flare pistol and put it away, and then I got a soda and went up to sit in the cockpit. It was another beautiful day, and I kicked back to relax and dozed off.

When a boat came in to dock two slips down, the rocking of my boat from its wake woke me up. I couldn't believe I had been asleep nearly four hours. I wouldn't be sleepy until midnight. I was just about to go below when I heard someone calling my name from the gate. I looked up to see a girl that I had dated a few time standing at the gate waving. As I walked up the dock to unlock the gate for her, I decided that the nap had been a good thing after all since I would probably be awake until midnight.

The next morning when I arrived at the track I couldn't decide whether to take the gun into the track or leave it in the truck. In the end, knowing how serious an offense it was to have a gun inside the track, I locked it in the truck. I couldn't bring myself to think that among all of these people someone would try to kill me.

The groom that James had talked to yesterday hadn't shown up for work this morning. That started the day off with grumbling from the ones who had to cover for him. Gene thought he knew someone he could hire as a replacement, who was a good worker and he left to find him. I hoped he didn't go into a trainer's shed row and steal one of his employees. That might cause me to get involved in a ruckus I wasn't looking for right now.

We had several to work this morning and I was about to go up to the grandstand when the last person in the world I wanted to see walked around the corner of the barn. He came straight to me, so he knew who I was, and put out his hand as he said, "I'm John Miller, Jodi Breaux's agent."

I hoped that my elevated blood pressure wasn't showing in my face as I took his hand and said, "How are you doing?"

"A couple of weeks ago you ran a first-time starter that I thought might make a runner. I'm trying to get Jodi on a few young horses so the guys can see that she gets along well with them. I would like a shot at riding that colt for you when you run him back." He had said all of this in a very pleasant way and in perfect English. I didn't hear any accent at all.

Under normal circumstances this would be a routine request from an agent. But the fact that I knew he didn't solicit mounts in the morning let me know this was no routine visit. I tried to play it the same as I would with any agent when I said, "I have already promised the jock that rode him in the first race the ride back. If I find I need to make a change, I will certainly give Jodi a chance. I like the way she rides."

He put out his hand again and said, "I would appreciate that." He turned to go and then turned back and said, "Let me give you one of my cards." He handed me one of his cards and turned to go again. He got to the edge of the shed row and turned one more time. "I watched the race on TV so I couldn't see very well, but I think I've met one of the owners somewhere before. St. German or something like that."

"Yeah, it's St. Germaine."

"I can't remember where I've met him. What kind of work does he do?"

"I don't have a clue. I have only had the horse for a month or two and I don't know them very well. I have twelve separate owners among my thirty horses, and I don't have any idea what any of them do for a living. It's something I never bother to ask. I have one owner that I know owns an auto parts store, and the only reason I know that is he sends my check every month from the store account."

He looked thoughtful for a minute and said, "It's not important. If your rider spins you or you are not satisfied with his next ride, give me a call." He turned and walked away, and I went in and sat down before I collapsed.

The guys had already sent three horses to the track so I hustled to the grandstand. I made it in time to watch the last half of their gallop and from there on the morning was back to normal. I didn't call Goodman right away, thinking I would wait until I left the track. Since I had no entries to make this morning, I followed the last horse back to the barn. A strange groom was giving a horse a bath while the hot walker held him, and I assumed this was the new man. I had never seen him around before and wondered where Gene found him.

James came into the office to give me the lowdown on the new groom. He apparently had worked for Gene at a small track in Ohio, and when Gene gave up and came home, the guy came to California with him. James said he seemed to know what he was doing, and he had hired him on two weeks probation. If he didn't work out, he would let him go. If Gene was sticking his neck out for him, I would bet the guy was competent. Gene never did anything that might make him look bad.

I had two horses running this afternoon and went to the kitchen for lunch. Afterwards I went out to my pickup for a little privacy and called Goodman. I related the morning meeting with Jon, and he didn't seem overly concerned about it. He thought Jon might be checking to see if they were the same people that had shown up on the roster of the FBI computer. He also would be checking to see if their owning a horse was a coincidence or somehow connected with their investigation. If he concluded it was connected, he would know he was blown and would probably disappear. He said I had played it just right and might have allayed his concern for awhile but not to relax my guard in case I hadn't satisfied him I wasn't involved.

The afternoon wasn't any better than the morning, and I didn't win either race. I had a second and a fourth, but the horse that ran fourth got trapped on the rail in the stretch and had nowhere to go. I thought he was the best horse in the race and if he hadn't got in trouble would have been right there at the end. You can't do anything about racing luck, and if you dwell on it you'll end up with ulcers.

I decided to go home for the night. I hadn't been there since Jon had been in it, and I was curious to see how he had left it. I stopped at a builders supply because I had seen an ad for a house alarm that hangs on the door and any movement sets it off. I talked to one of the store people, and he said the alarms worked great. Everyone that had bought one loved it. They were only twenty bucks and I got two, one for the door and one for the sliding door to my little balcony. I was on the second floor and didn't think anyone would be coming in that way, but for twenty bucks why not be sure.

I went through the apartment very carefully and could see no indication anyone had been there. I had expected him to be neat but thought it impossible I wouldn't see something amiss. When I didn't find any evidence of a search, it occurred to me that maybe he had come by to install some kind of listening device. I vowed to have no more conversations with Goodman from my home or my office. I even wondered if I should include my pickup in the no talk zones.

I walked down to the Subway sandwich shop on the corner for a meatball sandwich. I clipped the gun to my belt in the small of my back and didn't tuck my shirt in. I hadn't made up my mind yet whether I would eat in the shop or take it home but went early enough to be home before dark even if I ate at the shop. I didn't think I would wander around much after dark until this thing was over. Not even in my own neighborhood.

I ate at the shop and when I arrived back at the apartment, I hung the alarms and armed them. I had the thought while I was eating that if I was going to kill someone in their home I would hide in the house before they came home rather than break in after they were there. With my gun in hand, I went through every nook in the entire apartment and even looked under the bed. I had always considered horseracing to be a high stress business, but I was starting to realize I didn't even know what stress was.

The next morning I packed a few clothes to take to the boat before I went to the track. Even with the alarms I felt safer on the boat. I had about used up the clothes I kept on the boat and needed to refresh my supply. I had breakfast in my usual place and arrived at the track about the normal time.

It was a routine day and everything went according to plan. While I was in the grandstand, Goodman called me to ask how things were going. When I told him I didn't think I should talk to him from my home or my office, he agreed. He hadn't thought of the possibility of a bug and gave me an attaboy for thinking of it. I asked about the pickup, and he said that might also be bugged and we should limit our conversations to my mornings in the grandstand.

When I came back to the barn, I asked James how the new groom was working out and he liked him. He was quick and neat and knew what had to be done and did it. When I was finished with my paperwork, I walked down to his stalls and spent a few minutes talking with him. I didn't want him to think I was snubbing him because I hadn't been down to see him.

I only had one horse to enter today and didn't expect the race to go so I was in no hurry to get to the racing office. I finally ambled over to find out if they were using the race. I didn't care one way or the other. They didn't use the race but were bringing it back the next day as an extra. They were only one horse short of making the race and hoped one more day of rest would bring another horse or two.

My new gelding was in the second race and my second entry was in the sixth. I would get out of here at a reasonable hour, but I hated the two-hour wait between races. I went to the kitchen for lunch, but came back to the barn as soon as I finished eating. I had a couple of Forms I hadn't read yet, but I would regret it if I read them now instead of during the break between races. I was about to doze off sitting at my desk when the trainer from the barn next to me came in. They had just put out the new condition book for the next two weeks, and he brought me one. I would have plenty to do between races now so I read my Forms.

They called us over and we left for the receiving barn with our fingers crossed. The moment of truth was coming very soon.

When you're in the receiving barn with older, cheap horses, things are usually quiet. They have been to war so many times not much excites them. Today was no exception, and we were ready to go ahead of schedule. Of course they held us in the barn until proper time, but I had the groom just hold my horse in a stall. I didn't see any point in walking him for fifteen extra minutes. We went over to the saddling paddock, and my horse was acting the perfect gentleman so I left the saddling until the last minute. When the paddock judge started looking at his watch and glaring at me, I finally saddled him. I was just buckling the over girth when my rider came into the stall.

I normally don't give the rider too much in the way of instructions. I have found that they ride them pretty much however they have decided they are going to ride no matter what you say. Today I gave him just one instruction, "I am not sure how fit he is, so if he gets tired at the end, don't punish him."

They called riders up and we mounted and proceeded to walk around the parade ring. When we handed off to the pony boy, I was facing the tote board and our odds were thirty to one. I thought I might as well risk twenty dollars on a sixty dollar payoff. I am not a big bettor and make my money from winning purses, but when I see a horse way underpriced, I make a small bet on general principles.

I found a place to watch the race and put my glasses on the horse. He was warming up like a seasoned veteran and looked all business. I was glad of the way he was acting because the last two mornings he had galloped he had played around a lot and been kind of a handful. The odds had stayed near thirty to one the entire time and just as they started putting them in the gate the next tic of the tote board showed him at fourteen to one. Someone had dumped a ton of money on my horse, and I had no idea who it could be. The only thing I could think of was my friend from Pomona had a big time gambler on the hook. If you tipped the right kind of gambler and the horse won, they would give you part of the action; but I was surprised my friend had a connection like that. I knew my friend couldn't afford to bet fifty thousand dollars on a race, so it had to be a tip he had given someone.

They opened the gate and my horse broke sharp and went with the leaders. Going down the backside he was laying third about two lengths from the leader and running easy. He held his position through the turn even though the pace had picked up, and he was still running easy. About halfway down the stretch, the rider asked him to run, and he rolled right by the leaders. He opened up two lengths on the second horse and began to tire. When I saw his stride start to shorten, I thought we were too far from the wire to hold on, but no one else was coming and we coasted home by a length. Someone had just made a fortune on my horse.

The horse paid twenty-eight sixty and in fact someone had just made three quarters of a million dollars on my horse. I had no doubt that I would hear from the stewards as soon as they were told about the big wager. They would investigate to make sure I hadn't been involved in some kind of hanky-panky. They frowned on having scams run on the betting public, and the only thing that might save me a lot of grief was the fact that I had only owned the horse a month. It wasn't as if I had run him several times in bad races before I turned him loose. His form showed him to be a nice horse as a two-year-old, and he had two blistering works at Pomona. He paid big because he hadn't run in two years, but his works said he had come back ready to run. I would stand toe-to-toe with them if they called me in on it, and I was positive it was just a matter of time before they did.

I followed him to the test barn still trying to wrap my mind around someone betting fifty thousand dollars on one of my horses. The horse walked right into the test barn and right to the guys who gave the horses a bath. The thought flashed through my mind that this horse acts like he just ran two weeks ago and not two years ago. Then I had a horrible thought. Surely my friend wouldn't have run in a ringer on me, would he? Because of the huge wager, they would investigate that possibility along with everything else they could think of. All of a sudden, I wasn't nearly as pleased with my win as I had been a few minutes ago.

I forced myself to make it through the day and didn't even care that my second horse of the day wasn't in the money. I was more than a little worried about this new horse. If he turned out to be a ringer, my career was virtually over. As soon as I left the track, I grabbed my phone to call Pomona but stopped in mid-dial. If they pulled my phone records and the first person I called after his win was the trainer who had the horse until a few days before I ran him, it would be very incriminating. My best plan of action was to not do anything different from any other win. The term for a huge bet at the track was bridge jumper, and they were always placed on heavily favored horses and usually just to place or show. The term meant if you didn't win the bet you would jump off the nearest bridge. I have never seen a bridge jumper bet made on a thirty-to-one shot, and I'm sure the stewards haven't either. It was going to be hard to convince anyone that I had made two hundred and ninety dollars betting on my horse when someone had made nearly a million.

I was in such a confused state that I was halfway home before I remembered I was going to stay on the boat tonight. Since

I was already half way, I almost went on home but finally decided I should go to the boat. I stopped to pick up a pizza and only ate about half of it. I had suddenly lost my appetite.

I laid awake half the night going over the questions I thought the stewards were going to ask me and the best way to answer them. It was impossible for them to not think I was involved when I couldn't believe someone made a bet of that size without even asking me about the horse.

I came to the barn in the morning with a feeling of impending doom hanging over me. I went through the motions, but my mind was far away. I went to my place in the grandstand expecting to see security waiting for me. No one was waiting for me, but every time I heard the speaker system key up, I jumped, thinking this time they were calling for me. I was finally right about ten o'clock and they did call me. The message was short and to the point. "Chance Holden report to the stewards' office."

I was five minutes from their office, but it took me fifteen minutes to get there. I was trying to get my breathing and my heart rate under control before I reached it. I had thought of two or three hundred question they might ask me and was still caught totally off guard by their first question.

"Mr. Holden, are you acquainted with Gail Foster?" Up until now my name was Chance, but all of a sudden, I was Mr. Holden. That didn't look good for the home team.

"I don't think so. Give me a description of her."

"I had better not find out you are being a smart ass. If it turns out you know Mr. Foster, I will crucify you."

Jeez! I had gone to high school with a Gail Foster but I hadn't seen him in the twenty years since graduation. If it was the same person, I could kiss my butt good bye.

He interrupted my panic with the next question, "Are you acquainted with Mr. Ralph Finster?"

"The names not familiar, but I am acquainted with a lot of people that I don't know by name."

"These two gentlemen each placed a wager of thirty thousand dollars on a thirty-to-one horse yesterday—your horse. Do you know anything about that?"

"No sir, I don't, but I bet on him myself. On paper he looked like a good bet at thirty to one."

They all looked at each other to see if that revelation had the same effect on each of them.

"Would you share the size of your bet with us?" A sneer crept into his voice when he said it.

"Sure, I haven't cashed my ticket yet. I've got it right here." I reached in my shirt pocket and removed the ticket, "I bet twenty dollars."

The room went dead quite and the thought passed through my mind that I should cut out the cuteness and play this straight. I was going to have a tough enough job of convincing them of my innocence without pissing them off.

After a silence of a full five minutes while they collected their thoughts, the chief steward finally asked, "Are you willing to swear that you don't know Mr. Gail Foster or Mr. Ralph Finster?"

"No sir, I'm not. I am willing to swear that I don't recognize the names. Until I see them, I can't swear I don't know them by some other name like Speedy or Gimpy. I went to high school with a guy that graduated a year ahead of me by the name of Gail, but I don't remember his last name."

His voice was like chipped ice as he said, "You didn't go to high school with this gentleman. He's sixty-five or seventy-years-old." I can't tell you how relieved I was to hear that.

His next statement brought me back to reality with a jolt. "We are sending your blood test sample for a DNA test, and I promise you if it's not the correct horse you are going to jail. Is that clear enough for you?"

"Judge, we should get one thing straight up front. I am not involved in any kind of betting coup. I bought this horse a month ago at public auction. His tattoo matches, and other than that I don't know a thing about this horse. You just promised to put me in jail. I am going to make you a promise. I haven't done anything wrong, and if you say one word to anyone outside of this room indicating that I have and my reputation is damaged, I will sue all three of you for every cent that you have and every cent you earn for the rest of your life. Is that clear enough for you?"

He went tight jawed, but I have to give him credit: he held his tongue. "That is all for today, but I don't think this is over."

I said with some heat, "It damn well better be." I stalked out without a backward glance.

Training was about over and instead of going back to the grandstand I found a quiet place to call Pomona. When he answered I said, "Man you have got me in a real jam. Because of the big bets those guys made, they think I've run some kind of scam and they are threatening me with jail."

"Big bets what guys made? You're not making any sense."

"Are you telling me you didn't tout anyone on my horse yesterday?"

"I didn't mention him to a soul. I bet two hundred on him myself, but I didn't even tell the guys here at the track about him."

"Then this whole thing really doesn't make any sense. A guy named Gail Foster and a guy named Ralph Finster each bet thirty thousand on my horse yesterday. Do you know either one of them?"

"Neither one rings any bells with me. I thought the odds went a little crazy, but I was happy to make what I did and didn't pay much attention. Who could these guys be?"

"I have no idea, but I think I had better be finding out. Sorry I blamed you, but I couldn't think of any other reason someone would jump on my horse like that. I'll talk to you later."

I called Goodman and when he answered I said, "This is Chance and I need a huge favor."

"I'll try. What's up?"

"Yesterday I ran the horse I bought at the auction, and two guys, Gail Forster and Ralph Finster, each made bets of thirty thousand dollars. The horse won and they collected about three quarters of a million dollars. The stewards are accusing me of running a betting scam and threatening me with serious actions. I don't have the slightest clue who either one of these guys might be, but I sure need to find out. Is there any way you could find out something about them for me?"

"I don't see a problem with that. I'll run them through the computer and see what turns up. Call me back in a couple of hours."

"I appreciate it. I'll talk to you later."

I went back to the barn, but I was drained of emotion and just muddled around in the office for an hour, then walked to the kitchen for lunch where I had to put up with congratulations from several people on the win and the big payout. If they knew how much grief it was bringing me, they would stop with the congratulations. I waited for two hours on the dot and rang him back.

When Goodman answered I blurted. "It's Chance again. Did you find anything?"

"I found them both, but they seem legitimate enough. They own a thoroughbred breeding farm near Midway, Kentucky, and don't have any kind of a rap sheet. Forster had a speeding ticket ten years ago and nothing else shows up."

"Can you give me an address or a phone number for either one of them?"

"Sure. I can give you both a phone number and an address." He gave me the information and I wrote it down. "If there is anything else I can do to help, give me a call."

"No, this is more than enough, and I really appreciate it."

I picked up the phone to call the stewards and then a wild idea hit me. Instead of calling I went over to the racing office and asked to see his papers. It turned out to not be a wild idea after all. Ralph Finster and Gail Foster were the breeders of the horse and had raced him as a two-year-old when he was a nice allowance horse.

The stewards had already gone upstairs to the stewards' stand for the races, and their sectary transferred me. When you talk to the stewards on the phone, they always put you on the speaker so all three can hear the conversation, and it makes them sound as if they are in a barrel.

When one of them barked, "Stewards." I said, "This is Chance Holden, and I think I have solved the mystery."

After a pause one of them said, "We're listening."

"Finster and Forster were the breeders of the horse. They raced him as a two-year-old when he was a very good allowance horse. I am sure they thought that if he was sound enough to make it back to the races, he wouldn't have any problem handling a field of twelve-five claimers."

They muted the phone so I couldn't hear their conversation. When they put me back on, one of them said, "You're sure about this information?"

"I'm standing in the racing office with his papers in my hand."

"Are you ready to swear that you don't know either one of these people?"

"I don't know either one of these people, and I am going to give you their address and phone number so you can talk to them in person."

"How did you come by that information when we couldn't find anything on them?"

"Let's just say I know the right people to ask. Do you have your pen ready?" I gave him the information and then said, "I don't expect to hear from you again, but you know where to find me if you need more help." When the phone went dead, I said to myself, I'm a jerk. Why do I keep antagonizing these people when they have the power to make my life miserable?

I don't know if they ever called the guys or not. It was never mentioned again, and I was happy to have it behind me. The only thing that left a lingering worry in my mind was the possibility he would run a really bad race his next time back. That would put me in the spotlight again and lead to more questions. I didn't expect him to, but you never know what a horse will do.

Just in case I had left the impression we were both in trouble, I called Pomona to let him know who the guys were and that

I was pretty sure it was over. He sounded relieved and I was glad I had called. We talked a few minutes about the filly; he was thinking maybe two more weeks, and he would start sending her to the track. He said she was almost broke to lead properly and it had been a hassle from start to finish.

I started back to the barn and then decided the parking lot was closer. What the hell, they had got along without me all day why should I show up now? I pulled into a local restaurant to eat and was brought back to the present when a dark blue late model car pulled into the lot behind me and sat in the drive as if he wanted to see what I was going to do. After I parked I didn't spend any time in the parking lot. I went inside as fast as I could go without losing my dignity. I watched the door for ten minutes without anyone coming in. That really spooked me. Why would you pull into the parking lot of a restaurant if you weren't going in?

The place was close enough to the track that it drew horsemen and people I knew sat at two or three tables. I was trying to choose a table to force myself on when a trainer I knew passed me on the way back from the men's room. "Hey Chance, just walk in? Come sit at our table; we haven't ordered our food yet."

"Are you sure you don't mind?"

"You know everyone at the table; come on over."

"I knew track gossip was lighting fast and that everyone had probably heard about the bet by now. That was most likely the reason they wanted me to join them, but I wasn't going to volunteer anything. They were not going to get away with dropping hints either. By God, I was going to force them to come right out and ask me about it. If they wanted to play a game, then I would play my own brand of it.

I was nearly finished with my small steak when one of the guys finally gave up and asked me. "What was the deal on the bridge jumper on your long shot? I've never seen that before. That had to take large balls."

"I guess if money doesn't mean anything to you the balls don't have to be quite as large. It was two old guys from Kentucky who had bred and raised the horse. They had raced him as a two-year-old and won some money with him. They evidently are just senile enough to ignore the fact he hadn't started in two years. It paid off for them this time, but if they do that very often they will end up mucking stalls for somebody."

We had one more round of drinks and everyone was ready to break up the tea party. I wanted to be sure I left with the group because I didn't know who might be waiting in the parking lot. As we hit the parking lot, I was looking for the dark blue car, but it wasn't in sight. I was glad it was still daylight as I approached my pickup so I could see clearly into the area behind the seat. I had an extended cab with plenty of room behind the seat to hold a person. They had told me that some of these people had been killed by a garrote, and I wanted to be sure there was no one behind me when I got in the truck.

I did a couple of maneuvers that I thought were clever on the way to the boat. I pulled up in front of a little mom and pop grocery and went in for a six pack of soda. When I came out, I made a U-turn in the middle of the street and went in the opposite direction. Then I drove around in a residential neighborhood and suddenly pulled into a driveway in the middle of the block and backed out going back up the street to see what cars I met. I didn't see a dark blue car either time or any car that looked suspicious; I went on to the boat.

In all of the confusion of the last few days, I hadn't had time to look beyond a day ahead in the new condition book. Tonight was a good time for that, and I went through the book carefully, marking the races that I thought were right for my horses. It is a time-consuming task but kind of fun. Very often, I would find a race that fit two or even three of my horses and then it can be really difficult to decide which one to run in that spot. It is especially difficult if there hasn't been a race for either horse for a while. I finished about nine o'clock, and after making sure I was all locked in, I went to bed.

A lot of trainers are at the track by four o'clock in the morning, which means they have to get up before three. I don't even get out of bed until five and usually don't arrive at the track before six thirty. I have never understood what a trainer is thinking when he sends a horse to the track in the dark, but a lot of them do. I have always thought getting up at five as the downside of the business, and I'm sure I would change careers if I had to get up before three o'clock every morning.

I got to the track about normal time and found James and Gene sitting in my office going over the schedule for the day. It looked as if this was working out real well. They were even acting as if they were becoming friends.

The boys hadn't been to the barn since they had started investigating Jon, and I just assumed I should go on with their horse in a normal way. I hadn't scheduled him to work this morning, but I told James to send him five-eighths because I had found a race for him next week. Until I heard differently, he was just another horse in the barn. The morning went well and the boys' horse worked a little faster than I wanted, but he was feeling good, and the rider didn't fight him. He came back still playing, and I knew he was ready to run back.

A jock's agent that had ridden one of my horses in his last four races came up to where I was sitting. He was a good agent and was trying to mark the races in his condition book with the horses he would ride. He asked if I was going in a race he had seen that fit the horse and I said yes and he could ride him. He was still sitting next to me when Goodman called, and since I didn't want to talk in front of him, I told Goodman I would call him back in a few minutes. The agent asked about a couple of other races coming up that I had not made up my mind about and couldn't give him a definite answer. When he left I called Goodman.

"Hi, it's Chance. What's up?"

"It looks like our guy might be on the move. He booked a flight to Chicago for next week and his brother took a flight this morning."

"Why would the brother go a week early?"

"We've been kicking that around in the office and the consensus is that the brother is the lead scout. He follows the mark and gets his pattern and habits and Jon comes to do the deed. If the brother is spotted and/or stopped, he is a private investigator and has a client wanting the man checked out. He would take great care not to be armed or threatening in any way, and no one would suspect him of anything but what he says he is."

"That would explain how Jon always seems to have a lot of knowledge about the guy."

"Exactly. We are hoping that is his role because it will give us a clue to who the mark is. If we were blind we couldn't stop the assassination before it happened. We could only catch him afterwards. This may not only let us save his life, but we may be able to find out from the mark what the motive is and how he is involved with our bank of interest."

"Is your crew of watchers going on the plane with him?"

"Just one of them will go on the plane with him. We already have a team in Chicago that we deployed the minute the brother booked his flight, and they will keep him contained. We are assembling another team to wrap around Jon when he arrives.

It has to contain more than just watchers because when he makes his attempt he will have to be arrested, which could be a formidable job. Watchers are not pussy cats, but they aren't combat units either, and we will only get one shot at him."

"I hope this is the real deal. I'm ready to stop sleeping with a pistol under my pillow."

"I bet you are. I'll talk to you later."

"Oh, by the way, I am going to enter your horse for Wednesday. I'll call you if he gets in."

"Good, hopefully we can get away to watch the race. So long."

I was waiting for my last two horses of the morning to come on the track and thinking I could at last see light at the end of the tunnel. I sure hoped this went as easily as Goodman made it sound. I was tired of looking in my rear view mirror. I wanted this to be over.

The next few days were routine and uneventful. I hadn't any word from Goodman and I was still very watchful and cautious. He had said a flight next week but not which day. I would feel better when I knew Jon had left town.

I entered the boys' horse and he drew the four hole in the third race. I called Goodman to let him know and hoped he would be forthcoming with news, but he was not available. I left voice mail and asked him to call me. I spent the afternoon at the boat just lounging around and was disappointed when he didn't call me back.

The next morning I received two calls while I was in the grandstand and both times mistakenly thought it was Goodman. When training was over and still no word, I began to get a little worried. I hung around the barn an hour or two longer than necessary, thinking he might call or even stop by but to no avail. I went back to the boat and spent the afternoon thinking of every bad scenario that could have possibly occurred. I drove out of the marina to the little restaurant I eat at often and had dinner before going back to the boat, with still no phone call. I went to bed thinking bad thoughts and slept poorly.

In the morning I didn't exactly wake up. It was more like I came to. I was groggy as hell, and when I looked at my watch, it was seven o'clock. That woke me up like a bomb explosion; I leaped out of my bunk and started getting dressed like a mad man. I was half dressed before it dawned on me it was still dark outside. I looked at my watch again and realized it was twenty-five till eleven rather than seven. I felt like a fool as I got undressed and crawled back into my bunk. I was glad I was alone because I would never have lived that down.

When morning finally did come, I was exhausted and dragging around like a zombie. I had breakfast at my usual place and felt a little better by the time I reached the track, but it was going to be a long day. I had an even mix of workers and walkers scheduled and the morning went sour right away when the first worker pulled up lame.

I went down to take a look and met him at the gap as he came off the track. He had grabbed a quarter, which is something they ordinarily only do when they are breaking from a standstill. The rider said he was feeling good and had played hopscotch all the way from the barn to the track. That could account for him stepping on himself and barring an infection he would recover in a week or so.

I went back to the grandstand and called James to tell him how I wanted it treated. It was probably a waste of time because most grooms handle minor injuries however they were taught rather than how you tell them to do it. It wasn't too important how they treated it as long as they guarded against infection.

I watched the rest of training and made my notes before going to the racing office to make my entries. I was going to enter my auction horse this morning and prayed that he ran a credible race. He had won at twelve-five and I was going to try him at sixteen thousand this time. With his form as a two-year-old and his win the first time back, there was a possibility they would claim him for sixteen thousand. I was afraid if I jumped him any more than that, the stewards would be asking why I had run him so cheap the first time. I know they would claim him if I ran him back for twelve-five, and I wanted to see how good he was before I gave him away.

The vet had been at the barn when the horse that had grabbed a quarter came back from the track. He had cut off the flap that the toe grab had torn loose. I probably wouldn't have let him do that if I had been there, but it wasn't going to hurt anything. It might take a little longer to heal because it left more space that had to fill in. It was too late now to worry about it, but I had told James I wanted the flap taped down and a wrap put over it. Allowing the vet to cut it off wasn't the same as taping it down.

I went to the office for the draw, and when the horse came out of the box, I had to take a lot of ribbing from the agents. They all were asking how much I was going to bet this time. I didn't come back with any smart quips of my own. I wanted that episode behind me and hoped it would die quietly. I had caught a nine horse field and didn't recognize any monsters in the race. I might get lucky.

I went to the kitchen for lunch and had to take more kidding when the overnight came out and everyone saw he was in.

I didn't make any jokes here either. I took it all on the chin and hoped it would settle down soon. I had kind of hoped the boys would be there, but no luck.

I went back to the barn to wait for the race and suffered from attention disorder. I tried to read the Form, but I would catch myself reading the same paragraph four or five times without ever getting the gist of the article. I tried to do some work on my accounts, but I would add a column of numbers several times and get a different answer each time. I finally went back to the kitchen and watched a card game for an hour, and I couldn't tell you who was ahead in the game.

I was glad to hear them call us over for our race. I was pacing around the office like a caged animal and slowly going nuts. From there on I was going through the motions from habit and felt as if I was watching it on TV. When we came out of the saddling paddock to the parade ring, the boys were both there with big grins on their face. I shook hands and said hello, but we didn't have time to talk any. It was just as well because this wasn't the place to have the conversation I was interested in.

When the groom handed the horse to the pony boy, he still shied away a little but settled in beside the pony much quicker than before. The rider still cut loose from the pony to warm him up, but the pony picked him up after the warm-up and took him to the gate. He had learned from the first race and acted more like a veteran.

The first race had been six furlongs and this time I had put him in a six and one-half furlong race. He had acted like the extra distance might be good for him. He went in the gate without a problem and broke sharply.

He came away from the gate with the leader and laid just outside of him all the way down the back side. About midway through the turn, two horses made their move on the outside of him. I knew this was the moment of truth, and he would either wage war or give up. I was happy to see him shift gears and move with them as all three went by the front runner. The three horses were head to head until about the sixteenth pole and he suddenly started to move away. I couldn't tell if he accelerated or if they weakened, but he crossed the wire clear by two lengths and I was a happy camper.

The boys came into the winners circle with the attitude you would expect from a first time father. They couldn't have been happier if they had just won the Derby. It's always great to see a person's first win and how it affects them. They don't have a clue how many disappointments will follow, and they think this is the greatest game in the world. I was happy for them.

We took the picture and when the photographer asked them how many copies they wanted, I thought his eyes would pop out when they told him two dozen. The normal is one or two for the owner, one for the trainer, and one for the jock. He looked at me to see if they were kidding and I said, "They have large families."

The boys went back to the grand stand and I went to the test barn with the horse. I didn't figure to have this horse much longer, and I was glad to have gotten a win for them before it was over. For the first time today I felt good.

When I came back to the barn with the horse, the boys were waiting and of course wanted to go for dinner to celebrate. We went further from the track this time so we wouldn't be as likely to run into horsemen, but that didn't work very well. The first table we passed on the way to our table had three trainers sitting at it. I said hello as we passed but didn't stop to talk.

The boys were excited, and it took me awhile to understand that part of that excitement was because they had been taking a lot of lip from the guys they worked with. They had been the target of the whole group because they didn't know anything about horses and everyone was telling them they were being taken for a ride. They were going to put a win picture on each desk and start doing some trash talking of their own. I was happy for them.

It took a while for them to chill out and for the conversation to come around to business. I started it by asking, "When is Jon booked to fly out?"

Goodman as always was the talker of the pair. "He and his wife are on the red-eye Friday night. She is riding a horse on Sunday."

"Have they pinpointed who the brother is following?

"They have, but the brother is doing such a good job of shadowing him they haven't been able to approach him yet."

"So what do you intend to do now? You can't arrest him until he makes a move, and you don't know when he is going to move. What happens if he gets on the plane after the races Sunday and comes home?"

"We are totally convinced he is there to do a job. The only way he would just fly away without doing the job is if he smells us on his back trail. We are being very careful not to let that happen. We are using more people on this than anything we have ever done before. We have a team of over fifty people on this case so he will never see the same person twice. If he sniffs us out, he is the best there ever was. If he does sense us, he can't take a plane home because he'll know we have him tagged, and he will have to disappear. We sure aren't going to let that be the way this thing ends."

"I have one more question. What are you going to charge the brother with?"

"We've talked it over so many times we are sick of it, but the truth is we haven't come up with anything serious enough to keep him in prison more than a few years. We can only hope that when we spring the trap, he tries to help his brother fight his way out. If he is smart enough to just walk away, we aren't going to be able to do any real damage. Everything we have on him is circumstantial and very hard to prove beyond aiding and abetting."

"That's what I was afraid of. You never said whether you found the third M in the company name."

"We have a competent bunch of people going through the lives of these two guys all the way back to birth. If there is a third M, they will find him, but I have to admit they haven't yet."

The talk dwindled down to nothing and we decided to call it a day. I drove back to the boat to spend the night. Until Jon was on a plane out of town, I felt safer there. It was probably just an illusion, but nevertheless I was going with my feeling.

During the night a stiff wind came up and destroyed my hope for a good night's sleep. The boat moved and bumped the entire night and kept my imagination on full tilt. In normal times the moving of the boat would have been very peaceful, but these weren't normal times. It finally subsided about dawn and I had maybe an hour of rest before my alarm went off. This was going to be another long day.

On the way in, I didn't even feel like eating breakfast. I stopped and bought a bag of donuts and munched all the way to the track. I thought a sugar rush might get me moving—plus every now and then I just like to pig out on sweets.

I was a few minutes later than usual and had to park a long way out on the horseman's lot. I normally wouldn't have given it a second thought, but this morning it irritated me, and I knew I would have to be careful with my emotions today. A short fuse can cause you to do or say things that come back to haunt you later. Grooms tend to be sensitive to a fault about the way you treat them, and they never forget a slight, real or imagined.

The barn was in full swing when I arrived, and the first set of horses was already on the way to the track. I hustled up to the grandstand and in my haste forgot my binoculars. It was just another irritation to add to the list.

Things were going well and when my cell phone rang mid-morning, I answered expecting it to be Goodman. I was surprised when it turned out to be one of my owners. They almost never called me during training hours. He added a large irritation to my list by asking me to go look at a horse that was for sale. I didn't know the horse or the trainer that had him and didn't much like another trainer trying to sell one of my owners a horse without even giving me a heads up first.

I couldn't refuse to go look at him, but I wanted to. The owner already had three and seemed to be having trouble affording what he had. Another horse might be the preverbal straw. I got the trainer's name and his barn number and told him I would take a look after training.

When my last set of workers had gone, I decided that I was having a hard time staying awake and might as well walk on over and look at the horse. I only had four more to gallop, and they wouldn't miss me. I found the barn easy enough but had trouble finding the trainer. He only had three horses and no one stabled in his barn knew him very well. A hot walker suggested he might be in the kitchen so I walked over to check. The irritations were adding up.

I found him in the kitchen in a card game. Another irritation, as I had to wait for the game to be over before we could go look at the horse. When the game ended I could see him struggle with the idea of asking me to wait for one more game. He had no way of knowing how quick I would be out of here if he did. That was an irritation that wasn't going to be added to my list today. His better judgment prevailed; he paid off and got up.

On the way to the barn, he started his sales pitch. "This horse has been running well and I hate to sell him, but I need the money. I have started him four times at the meet and he has hit the board every trip"

"What kind of price have you been running him for?"

"I've been running him for twenty-five thousand. He should be a bargain for the twenty I'm asking for him. He is sound and dead fit. You could enter him today."

We reached the barn before I could start asking questions, and I didn't see any point in asking any more until I had looked at the horse. He led him out of the stall and I walked around to get a side view first. He wasn't a bad made horse, but he was on the small side. I have had some runners that were small, but I prefer them larger. It was when I went to the front view that I lost interest in the horse. He was crooked in both front legs from the knees down. He might be sound now but the chances of him staying sound were very slim. The ankles and knees take such a pounding in a race horse that if they don't align with the ankle under the knee you have almost no shot at holding him together.

I spent another ten minutes looking at the horse so he couldn't tell my owner that I didn't give him a proper inspection and told him I would call my owner and discus it with him. I said I was on my way to make an entry and would call my owner as soon as I got back to the barn.

When I got to the racing office, I asked one of the entry clerks to look up the horse for me. She turned the screen around for me to look at his race record. He had made five starts instead of four and only the first two had been for twenty-five. The last three had been for twenty and he had one third and one fourth from the five starts. If he was going to lie about things that were easily checked, it was fairly certain he was going to lie about everything else. If my owner bought this horse, he would need a trainer for him. I wanted no part of him.

It was a struggle, but I made it through the day without falling asleep, or even worse, blowing up at someone. I was watching the clock as if I worked in a factory. I discovered what every factory worker knows at an early age: The hands on a clock move very slowly when you would rather be somewhere else. I thought the day would never end and started several times to tell James that he was in charge for the rest of the day. I only held off on doing that because I like to save it for days when I really need to be gone. A lot of trainers spend very little time at the barn, but I'm not one of them.

When it was finally time to leave, I was the first one ready to walk out of the barn, but then I remembered I hadn't called my owner about the horse he asked me to inspect. I said a few choice words under my breath and called to give him my report. He adopted an attitude that made it sound as if I hadn't given the horse a fair chance, and it took all of my will power to stay civil. I explained that the guy was not truthful about his race record, and the horse had run three times for twenty thousand with no takers. He had not hit the board for twenty-five as the trainer had claimed and had barely hit the board two out of his three starts for twenty. I recommended that he not buy the horse and because I was in a foul mood did not go on to say I wouldn't train him. If that took a bad turn with the mood I was in, I would probably lose a client. I would save that for a day when I was feeling more tactful.

On the way to the boat, I called ahead for a pizza and picked it up for dinner. I ate half of it with a soda and locked myself in for the night. I was exhausted and planned to sleep for ten hours.

My next conscious thought was the alarm clock was chirping in my ear. I had slept a full ten hours without interruption and hoped I was back to normal. I would have enough on my mind today without worrying about my energy level. My auction horse had better run a decent race, and Jon had better get on that plane tonight. That was enough anxiety for one day. I didn't need anything more.

I had a good breakfast on the way to the track and arrived feeling good only to have unwelcome news waiting for me. My farrier informed me that he was retiring at the end of the meet. This was a problem for me because I insist that the farrier use a hoof gauge when my horses are shod, but most of the farriers refuse to use one because it slows them up.

I have always thought being a racetrack farrier is like having a license to steal. The horses are shod so often that there isn't much trimming involved. For the most part, they just rasp the foot off smooth and nail the new shoes on. It takes them about a third of the time it takes to shoe a regular horse, and they charge twice as much for the job. They have a good union so you play their game or you don't play.

I have never understood how a group of independent businessmen can be allowed to have a union. That is actually a cartel, which is supposed to be illegal. At the tracks where they don't have a union, they are in collusion to hold their prices, which is also supposed to be illegal. No matter how you label it, there is something illegal about the artificially high prices you must pay to have a horse shod on the racetrack.

The problem is the toe grows faster than the heel. When they rasp the foot, they set the rasp flat on the foot, taking the same amount off of the entire foot. You eventually end up with a long toe and no heal. Many of the trainers think this gives a horse better traction and will help them run faster. I don't know about that, but I do know it puts a lot more pressure on his knees, ankles, and tendons and it is not natural. Most of the horses on the track have little or no heel, and I have found the only way to keep that from occurring is to insist they use a hoof gauge, which shows you the angle of the foot. As much as they charge for their services, you would think they could spend five more minutes on the job; but most of them refuse.

I have thought about this problem before, and if no one will agree to use the gauge, I am going to try an end run. I have talked to one of the farriers at the polo grounds about it, and he doesn't have a problem with using a hoof gauge. I am going to put him on the payroll as a groom and have him shoe my horses. I think the union will try to stop me, but I'm not sure I don't have the right to do that. I also like this guy's shoeing. You don't see any horses with no heels at the polo grounds.

Other than the bad news about my farrier, the morning went splendidly, and we were finished by nine o'clock. I didn't have anything to enter for Sunday so I had a couple of hours to kill. I walked to the kitchen and sat down in a card game that was just starting. I played one game very badly and decided that I was spoiling the game for everyone else by my lack of concentration so I quit. I bought a Form and went back to the barn.

I turned to my race in the Form and checked to see what kind of competition I was facing. I was listed as second favorite at three to one, and looking at the past performances of the horses, I agreed with the odds. There was only one horse that I wasn't sure I could beat if my horse ran his best race.

The last work on my horse showed a minute flat for the five-eighths. The clocker had added a second to the work, as he had actually gone fifty-nine flat. My rider knew she had gone faster than I wanted and had waited at the barn for me to explain that she had not asked him to run. He had done it on his own and so easily she didn't realize how fast he was going. The benefit of watching your horses work was that I knew she was telling the truth.

One of the reasons I suspected I might lose the horse today was that when they announced he was about to work, four trainers went to the rail to watch him. Two of those trainers had their own watch and would know he worked faster than the time the clocker had posted him as working. I would be sorry to lose him, but I had learned a long time ago that refusing a profit on a horse was a rookie mistake and over the long run would cost you a lot of money. A racehorse is a perishable commodity that at all times is only a heartbeat away from a career-ending injury that would render him worthless. John Madden, who I consider the best horseman that ever lived, is quoted as saying, "Better to sell and repent than keep and resent." I would have phrased it a little differently, but you get the point.

The wait for my race allowed me to catch up on the paperwork I had been neglecting for the last few days; that kept me occupied until race time and made the waiting pass quickly.

As we walked over to the receiving barn, I noticed a couple of assistant trainers standing outside with cell phones in their hand. This was a sure sign that one of the horses was on the claiming radar of at least two trainers. The assistants were there to get a last look at him before the claim was dropped. If they didn't spot anything to make them suspicious, they would phone their OK to someone at the claiming box to drop the claim. It wasn't necessarily my horse, but I suspected that it was.

We went through the saddling routine without any problems, and as I legged the rider up I told him I thought we were going to lose the horse and to make every effort to win the race. An experienced rider knows the difference between saving a horse to leave something for his next race and going all out when there is no tomorrow.

As the horses warmed up and went toward the gate, I watched the tote board, praying there would be no bridge jumper bet made on him. I was relieved when they loaded in the gate and the odds stayed at four to one. At least I wouldn't have to fight that battle again.

They opened the gate and my horse broke sharp. He went with the leader, who happened to be the favorite, and laid right on his hip all the way down the backside. He eased up to head and head through the turn, and as they straightened out in the stretch, he went on by. I hoped he hadn't made that move too early, but I didn't need to worry as he won by a widening two lengths and was never threatened. The favorite faded to third and the second place horse was dying at the end. The stewards had no cause to hassle me about anything concerning this race, and I felt a huge weight lifted from my shoulders.

In the winner's circle I was surprised to see Goodman and St. Germaine waiting to have their picture taken with me. I had just gotten rid of one of my anxieties, and I sure hoped they weren't here to tell me Jon had canceled his flight. They both seemed happy enough and were all smiles as the picture was taken.

When the horse was unsaddled and was being led away to the test barn, the clerk of scales handed me a claim slip. I had already faced the fact I was losing him so it didn't come as a shock; but there was always that little glimmer of hope until they actually handed you the slip. I guess if you can't be happy about a sixty-day profit of over forty thousand dollars on an investment of four thousand, you won't ever be happy.

James had come to watch the race and I asked him to go to the test barn with the horse while I visited with the boys. I tried to find us a spot with a little privacy, but that's hard to do at the track during races. I was steeling myself for bad news and was relieved when Goodman said, "We just happened to be in the area and thought it would be fun to watch the race. Remember, we were with you when you bought this horse, and we feel a connection to him. He ran a great race."

I felt better already as I said, "He ran a very good race, but they claimed him from me."

The news sobered them up and took some of the fun out of the win. Goodman said, "Oh, that's too bad. Did you expect that?"

"I was about ninety percent sure they would, but you always have that ten percent of hope they won't."

"Could you have run him for more?"

"I could have, but I was kind of in a trap. After the stewards gave me such a bad time about the huge bet placed on him in his first race, I was afraid if I jumped him to twenty-five they would go back to thinking I was in on the bet. It's near impossible to defend yourself against appearances. If something appears to be rotten, the stewards assume it is until you prove otherwise. I just didn't want to open that can of worms."

"I see your point, but it cost you a nice horse."

"I can always buy a horse—all it takes is money—but I was starting to like this one. You guys didn't bring me any bad news, did you?"

"No. This was strictly a social visit. We just wanted to watch his race."

"I'm glad about that. Are you coming back to the barn?"

"No, we are playing hooky for a couple of hours, but that is all the time we can spare. I will call you in the morning to tell you if Jon boarded the plane."

"It was nice of you to come by, and I ordered you each a copy of the win picture. I'll give them to you the next time I see you. How did the win pictures of your horse go over around the office?"

"We made every one of them eat a double serving of crow. I haven't had so much fun since I was in college. Even St. Germaine put in a few licks. It was great."

We shook hands and they headed for the parking lot. As I walked back to the barn, I couldn't help thinking I would miss them when this was over. I had grown to like them both, but that didn't keep me from hoping it was over. I had enough of looking over my shoulder, and being afraid to go home. I was looking forward to the days of old when my main worry was that one of my horses would come back from the track lame.

When James and the groom came back from the test barn, they both were a little down. This was a normal reaction when a horse was claimed, even if you didn't particularly like the horse. In this case they liked the horse, and that made it worse. You would think that with as much claiming as goes on around a race track you would become immune to that low feeling when you lose one, but you never do.

We put our equipment away and locked up before leaving for the day. I decided to spend one more night at the boat since Jon hadn't left town yet. On the drive to the marina, I stopped and ate a good diner and already felt more relaxed than I had in several weeks. I even thought about taking the boat out for a late afternoon sail but in the end decided I was too lazy. I watched TV for a couple of hours and went to bed early.

I awoke before the alarm went off, feeling well rested for the first time in days. Since I was early, I made my own breakfast and took my time eating and cleaning up afterwards. I drove to the track with nothing on my mind but business and horses for the first time since this thing had started. I refused to consider that Jon may not have gotten on that plane.

The morning went off fairly routinely except one of the grooms got kicked in the thigh. It didn't do any real damage, but he was going to have a hell of a bruise. Many of the grooms do their stalls with the horses still in them, and I have never understood why they don't get kicked more often. They make the horses move out of their way as they work around the stall, and some of the horses get to the point of moving on voice commands. This particular time the groom had reached out to move the horse's rear without warning and surprised the horse. His reward for the mistake was a badly bruised thigh.

I went to the track with my first horses and had only just made it to the grandstand when my cell phone rang. It was Goodman with the news that Jon had indeed made the flight and was out of my life for the time being. I had refused to consider any other outcome, but I was still relieved to hear the news.

For some reason the day seemed brighter and my horses all looked as if they were feeling tiptop. The workers worked sharply and the gallopers were playing and full of energy. It was amazing how little it took to make a guy like me happy. I might even go out for a couple of drinks tonight. I had gone without female companionship for so long I was starting to feel like I was qualified to take confessions. I am definitely not cut out for the life of a monk.

I went on the prowl at one of the clubs at the marina and made a new friend. I had a pleasant evening and came to work the next morning feeling at peace with the world. One of the great things about California is the women are as aggressive as the men so making a new friend is never a problem.

It was a normal Saturday morning with a few of my owners showing up to watch training. It is a rare Saturday that I don't have at least a couple of them come to the barn, and I always have a fresh pot of coffee and two or three boxes of donuts ready.

The owner who had me check out the horse was in the group that came today. He wanted to see the horse for himself, and I gave him the option of going over alone or waiting until after training when I could go with him. He opted to go alone, and I cautioned him against buying the horse without having a vet check first. I didn't want him to make a snap decision based on the trainer's sales pitch.

The other three owners that came were there just to watch the horses and soak up the racing atmosphere. They always seemed to enjoy feeling like they were part of the team and if you weren't careful would get in the way. They all wanted to do hands-on things and not knowing a lot about horses needed watching at all times. It would be a bad thing if you let one of them get hurt or do something that would cause one of the horses to get hurt. Saturdays are never dull and sometimes are even fun, but I am always glad when they are over.

The afternoon was a downer though. I had two horses in and the first one stumbled coming out of the gate and dropped his rider. The second one ran a bad fifth with no excuses and proved again that we were running him above his pay grade. If I could convince the owner of that, this horse had the potential to make some money. As it stood now, we were just filling races for the track with no compensation for our efforts.

I didn't allow the poor showing of the afternoon to dampen my good mood. I left the barn telling the crew that tomorrow would be a better day. I knew I wouldn't have any bad races because I didn't have anything in.

The owner that went off to look at the "for sale horse" never came back to the barn. I wanted to know what the status was on that deal, so on the way home I gave him a call. He was a little vague about the horse but ended by saying he didn't like him enough to buy him. I dodged a bullet there and could put that problem to rest.

I just made the cleaners before closing time and exchanged a bag of dirty laundry for my clean laundry. I have a washer and dryer in my apartment and the marina has a washer and dryer on the dock, but I tend to procrastinate to the point of running out of clean cloths. I have found it is simpler to have my laundry done, and it isn't that expensive. I went home and sorted out the clothes that went back to the boat, and put the rest of them away.

I went to the barn Sunday morning still feeling on top of my game. I was looking at half a day because I didn't have anything running. I had promised to take my new friend from Friday night sailing this afternoon. She had never been sailing and was eager to go. The only problem with that scenario was experience had taught me that about fifty percent of first-time sailors get sea sick. I had a fifty-fifty chance of having a good time and a fifty-fifty chance of losing a friend. Once you have seen them puking over the side, they are too embarrassed to go out with you again. I always look on the good side and tell myself that half of them love it.

The morning was uneventful but the afternoon made up for it. She was a natural sailor and loved it. She had heard of the mile-high club but had never heard of the mile offshore club. I allowed her to join it anyway. I didn't want her to miss a chance to join an elite club.

We made the harbor just about sunset and we were both tired. She had met me at the boat, which meant she had her own car. I explained that I had an hour or two of cleaning up and sent her on home. I took my time and did a thorough job because I didn't know when I would be on the boat again. By the time I finished cleaning her up and tying everything down, it was getting late and I headed for home.

I was pulling into the garage when my phone rang. I had barely said hello before Goodman boomed in my ear, "Where in the hell have you been? I've been calling you for two hours."

I was taken aback by his tone and said, "I've been sailing and phone towers are in short supply out there. What's up?"

"I need to see you right away. Where are you now?"

"I just drove in the driveway at home. What's up?"

"Jon got away from us. I'll be right over. Don't leave your apartment." He hung up on me.

The tone of his voice and the staccato manner of his talking left no doubt in my mind that he was really shaken. My first reaction was panic, but then as I sat in my truck thinking about it, I realized that Jon was in Chicago and I was in Southern California. I was in no immediate danger and could wait to hear what Goodman had to say. Then I would panic.

It was a full hour before Goodman knocked on my door, and I had grown increasingly nervous. With my gun in hand, I asked who it was before I opened the door. When Goodman identified himself, I opened the door to find him disheveled and obviously stressed out. Just his appearance alone was enough to put my nerves on edge. I knew this was very bad.

He came in, sat down, and lit a cigarette. I didn't even know he smoked. I got him an ashtray and sat down across from him and waited while he collected himself.

"This is the damnedest thing I have ever seen." he finally said, "This guy is unbelievable."

When he showed no sign of going on, I asked, "What happened?"

"We had this building sewed up tighter than Fort Knox. Keep in mind this is not a hotel, where people can come and go at will. This is a high-rise condominium on Lake Front Drive. It is an exclusive building with guarded access and security cameras everywhere. You can't enter the building unless a resident has left your name with the security desk. There are no exceptions.

"The mark lived on the fourth floor in a unit in the middle of the building. We had two of our people in the unit with him. There was a unit across the hall and two doors down that was not being used because the owners were in Florida. We had set up our command center there, with a tie in to all of the security cameras. We had four men in that room and one of them was monitoring the cameras at all times. We had a bank of computer monitors set up that would allow uninterrupted coverage of all cameras. We had four men in two cars at every entrance and exit of the building, including the fire escapes. We had two snipers on the roof of every building with a view of the protected building. We had two men patrolling the hall of the floor above and of the floor below. We didn't think a mouse could enter or leave without our permission.

"We had two people watching Anders, who was sitting in a coffee shop on the corner, and we had a tail on Jon so we knew where he was. What could go wrong?"

"I am guessing that something went very wrong."

"You won't believe how this thing played out. I think Anders must be the brains behind this group because Jon strikes me as a reactor rather than a planner. But whoever planned this should be a general in the military. He has missed his calling. The plan allowed for every contingency that could possibly occur.

"To begin with Jon went into his hotel, and the tail could do nothing but wait for him to come out. The hotel was completely covered, with men at every exit. With Jon in his hotel, maybe the coverage of the condo relaxed a little, but not much. How Jon got out of that hotel without anyone spotting him we may never know; but he did.

"Next he managed to make the fourth floor of the apartment complex without showing up on any camera. We don't know how he did that either, but obliviously he knew where every camera was located.

"Now comes the unreal part. He had an entry card to the apartment we were using as a command center. We think he was going to use the unit himself to set up for his hit. The command center was set up in the dining room and no one had a view of the front door. The average guy, when he discovered how the unit was being used, would have backed out and disappeared. Instead Jon walked in on our people and put all four of them down with head shots. He must have recognized they were wearing vests and didn't waste a single shot on their torsos. Three of them were killed and the fourth is not expected to survive.

"At this point you would expect him to make a hasty retreat, realizing he had walked into a trap. Instead he calmly walked down the hall and using a card key for that door, walked in and dispatched our two agents and the mark. They couldn't have known he was even in the building and not one of their guns was drawn. We now have seven down and not one of their weapons is out of the holster.

"Now comes the superior planning that we didn't suspect. He made his way to the fire escape at the end of the hall and proceeded to come down. The two teams guarding the fire escape saw someone on the fire escape and having no idea who it was, got out of their cars to investigate. There had been no alarm up to this point and they may have been a little careless, but I doubt the outcome would have been any different if they knew it was him. In the building facing the fire escape, a sniper in one of the apartments cut all four of them down in the street without them even knowing where the shots were coming from. He had killed all four of our agents before one of our snipers located him and took him out.

"In the distraction of our snipers' frantic searching for the sniper who was shooting our agents, Jon was able to reach the ground and disappear into the adjacent building. The sniper turned out to be a guy who had worked on Jon's crew when he was in South Africa. Since he had a night scope with him, we assume the original plan had been for Jon to stay in the unit we were using as a command center until dark. When he discovered it was a trap, he reacted with deadly violence. We couldn't find any transportation for either one of them and so we assumed they had come together, and Jon just drove away in the car they had arrived in.

"It was a total fiasco. We had nine agents killed, one dying, and the mark, who we were counting on to make a connection to the bank for us, killed. All we have to show for it is a dead sniper that we didn't even know existed before today, and a private detective we may not be able to connect to the crime. There is going to be hell to pay for this."

"Is the private detective Anders?"

"Yes, and It is a miracle he didn't get away also. He was wearing an ear bud that we thought was a blue tooth for his phone. It turned out to be a direct connection to Jon. As soon as Jon alerted him of the trap, Anders calmly got up and left the coffee shop. Remember, no one had sounded an alarm as yet, and he nearly evaded his tail because they weren't expecting any evasive moves. We were lucky to catch him, but we are going to need even more luck to hold him. With Jon not being caught, we are going to have a tough time proving it was Jon at the crime scene. The only thing we caught on any camera was the back of a man in a business suit entering the condo of the mark and exiting the condo four minutes later holding a newspaper in front of his face. Although we are checking for finger prints, we don't expect to find any. Everyone who saw him is dead or dying, and if we can't prove it was Jon, it will be impossible to hold Anders. The biggest crime of all will occur if they get away with this."

"Wow! Was this all done with a twenty-two?"

"No, he used a nine millimeter for this job, and we suspect he used two guns. He took the time to police his brass, so we can't be sure about that until ballistics is finished with the slugs. The gun or guns were obliviously fitted with silencers because no one heard a single shot. Even the sniper's rifle was silenced. Part of the reason Jon was able to escape was that none of our people were even aware anything was going on. He was out of the building before the first alarm was sounded."

"I assume he didn't go back to his hotel."

"He has disappeared without a trace. His wife was at the race track, with a mount in a race, and has no idea what we are even talking about. At this point she thinks we're making this up. She refuses to believe any part of the story. The people interviewing her tend to think she is telling the truth. If that is the case, she is not going to be of any help whatsoever.

"We have the largest manhunt we have ever mounted in place. We are covering every known exit out of the country. We are watching all border crossings as well as every place where he could catch a plane, train, bus or boat. We even have agents at small, local airports checking private planes. If a plane is large enough or close enough to make it to any border, we want to see who is on board before it takes off.

"I think we are going to spend our entire yearly budget on this project, and in a very short time. I shudder to think of the repercussions if he slips through our fingers. We are backed against the wall and in the position of feeling we have to catch this guy just to prove our viability. If we allow a person who we had under twenty-four hour surveillance to walk in and kill ten people and walk away untouched, it will put a stain on the Bureau that may never be erased."

"I can see your point, but if he had an exit plan already in place, he may already be gone."

"That is exactly what we are afraid of, but it doesn't make sense. He has been doing this successfully for ten years and we can't believe he had an exit strategy in place every time. He had no way of knowing this time would be different, and we hope he didn't have a plane standing by. On the other hand, it is hard to believe he has had the sniper protection in place every time over the last ten years, but it was there the first time he needed it to be. I have to admit this guy has the entire Bureau perplexed. If Elvis has truly left the building, we have some people at the Bureau who will need to be put on suicide watch."

"Where do I stand in all of this? Do you think he will come after me?"

"There are a couple of reasons that I don't think you are in any danger. First, there is nothing to indicate that you have been involved with any of this. I can't imagine that he could, or would, connect you to what happened in Chicago. Second, he has never shown any desire for revenge. Every hit has been at a very professional level, and nothing has ever indicated anything personal. That being said, we plan to keep an eye on you for the time being, to insure your safety. We owe you at least that much."

"Do you think I would be safer here or on the boat?"

"Each place has advantages and disadvantages. I would suggest you choose the location where you feel safest. I wouldn't bounce back and forth because our people will be faced with different problems at each location. It will make it easier for them to keep an eye on you at just one place."

"OK, I think I will stay on the boat. I feel safer there, and I think it will be easier to see him approach if he does come after me. I'll move down there tomorrow after I finish at the track."

"I'll relay that to our watchers. There is one more thing I want to give you. This little pendant and chain might save your life. Wear it around your neck and all you have to do to send an alert to the watchers is press it. In fact it will alert more than just the watchers. It will send a signal to every agent in the city. Don't make the mistake of crying wolf because it will draw an army of very dangerous people, and they won't be happy."

"You make me afraid to wear it. What happens if I accidently bump it against something?"

"I don't know. I would suggest you guard against doing that."

"Thanks a lot."

"I'm joking. When you press it, you will hear a beep. If it is pressed by accident, when you hear the beep, you have ten seconds to cancel it by pressing it twice."

"That sounds more like it. You'll have to pardon me if my sense of humor has worn a little thin right now."

"I understand, and I can't blame you. I also think you should take advantage of your gun permit and never be unarmed."

"I was thinking the same thing."

"I guess we have covered everything I came to tell you. We have no reason to believe he will return to Los Angeles, but we will be vigilant. He hasn't done anything we have expected so far, and we are getting tired of being behind at every step. Get some sleep. I'll call you if I hear any news."

I let him out and locked the door behind him. I made sure all of the windows were covered and turned out most of the lights. I didn't think a sniper rifle would give me a pleasant experience. I had to agree with Goodman that he shouldn't have any reason to come after me, but I also had to agree with him that Jon had been a step ahead of them at all times. It was hard to believe that two or three guys could make a fool out of the largest investigative organization in the world. I had no intention of underestimating Jon or his connections.

I normally can fall asleep anytime I get quiet. In fact I have a tendency to fall asleep driving and have had several minor and one serious accident because of this. I knew that this was going to be the second sleepless night I had suffered because of Mr. John Miller. I hoped they shot him just to make him pay for that. I don't know how insomniacs can stand to be exhausted and not able fall asleep. I would have to be committed within a week. When the alarm went off, I may have been asleep longer than I thought. I was sure I was still awake and when the alarm sounded I knew something was amiss. It took a couple of minutes to get my bearings and realize it was five o'clock in the morning. The last time I had looked at my watch it was before midnight. I must have been dreaming that I was awake. That's kind of scary, don't you think.

I wasn't nearly as tired as I had expected to be and even had a good appetite when I stopped for breakfast. But when I reached the barn, the morning went to hell quickly. The trainer that had tried to sell my client a horse was pacing up and down in my shed row. I could see he was in a rage and tried to avoid trouble by saying in a pleasant voice, "Can I help you?"

He snapped back, "You better try to help yourself because I'm going to whip your ass."

I still was trying to diffuse the situation as I said in a still pleasant voice, "And that would be because?"

"Because you told the guy that was going to buy my horse that he was no good."

The pleasantness went out of my voice as I said, "Look pal," and I bit down on the word pal, "A man is entitled to his opinion and mine is that your horse is a crooked-legged piece of junk looking for a place to break down. I wouldn't recommend him to my worst enemy and certainly not to one of my clients."

I walked over and picked up the phone as I said, "If you are not out of my shed row in ten seconds, I will call security and have you put out of my shed row and off of the racetrack."

He got so red faced I thought he was going to have a stroke as he said, "If you don't put down that phone, I am going to cram it down your throat."

At that instant Gene walked up, and as I mentioned before, he is a big boy. He said, "No need to call them boss; I've already called. They are on the way"

I could see the indecision in his eyes. He knew if the stewards at one track ruled him off for fighting, he would be ruled off everywhere, but he hadn't decided yet if that was important enough to matter right now. I didn't say anything to antagonize him or to sooth him. I was at the point of not caring which way he jumped. He was way over the line, and I was going to leave the outcome up to him.

He was still straddling the fence when two security people in a golf cart pulled up in front of the barn. As they got out of the cart, he backed up a couple of steps but was still close enough to hit me if he lost it so I didn't take my eyes off him.

"What's the problem here?"

I didn't know what might come out of his mouth so I spoke first, "This gentleman is upset because I recommended that one of my clients not buy a horse he has for sale. He stopped by to let me know he thinks I am a jerk."

"Has he threatened you?"

"Just by the fact that he is visibly upset. I would like him out of my shed row, but he hasn't said everything he wants to say yet, and won't leave."

The security man turned to the trainer and said, "Let me see your license please."

He handed him his license, and as the guard wrote down his name and badge number, the trainer looked at me and I could see he was not cooled off yet. I had tried to do him a favor, but it might have been a mistake. If I had given a true account of his actions, he would be in the stewards' office first thing in the morning.

After the guard handed back his license, he spoke for the first time, "How come you haven't asked for his license?" The venom was apparent in his voice, and it brought the security guard's head up.

The guard looked at him for a long minute before he said, "Sir, let me give you a little advice. I know that this gentleman just gave you a get-out-of-jail-free card. If I were you, I would get the hell out of here before I decide to take it away from you. I see plenty of witnesses to ask tell me what really happened. Now use a little common sense and go back to your own barn."

The trainer glared at the security guard for a minute and then turned on his heels and stomped away. After watching him out of sight, the guard turned back to me and said, "Do you think he is finished?"

"I think he probably is. He said the other day that he was shipping to Ohio today. Maybe we'll be lucky and he really is leaving."

"If he comes back, give us a call and we'll help him leave."

"Thanks Tony. Sorry to have bothered you."

"No bother. Just call if he comes back."

We returned to the business of training, and I went to the grandstand. We had more workers than usual today and they take a little more time so we still had a couple of horses on the track at closing time. In fact I was the last one off of the track and the outrider, who had to wait for the horse to come off the track, glared at me like I was spoiling his day. I felt like saying, if you want a piece of me, take a number.

We finished at the barn about noon, and since I had loaded extra clothes this morning, I went straight to the boat. I could use a few groceries, but I didn't feel like picking them up today. Tomorrow was another dark day and I would shop then. The new condition book had come out today, and I planned to spend the afternoon picking races for my horses and relaxing.

I had just opened my condition book when my cell rang. I thought it would be Goodman with the latest news, but it was my friend from Pomona. "Hey, did you forget about this filly, pard?"

I didn't want to admit it, but with all that was going on, I had forgotten about her. "I've been really snowed under and I figured I would hear from you when you had something to tell me. I didn't want you to think I was looking over your shoulder."

"I think I've done as much as I can. She has learned a few manners and is starting to understand what is expected of her. She worked this morning in a minute and two and change. As slow as this track is right now, that was a good move. In fact it was the second fastest of the day."

"I'll pick her up tomorrow after training if you feel she is ready to come to the races."

"I think she's ready, but I wouldn't recommend betting fifty thousand on her next start."

"You really know how to hurt a guy. I'll see you tomorrow about noon."

I closed my phone and tried to picture the filly in my mind. I had an empty stall with the other horse being claimed, and I would bring her over and give her a try. I had paid very little for her and didn't intend to fool with her too long. If she didn't show me that she could compete with these horses, I would find her a new home. The fair circuit would be starting in a couple of months and that was about the maximum amount of time I would invest in her. If she didn't fit here, I would let someone going to the fairs take her, with instructions to get her claimed or to sell her. The bottom claiming at the fairs was so low that if she couldn't win there she wasn't worth feeding.

I had reopened my condition book when the phone rang again. This time it was Goodman. "What's going on?"

"Nothing, I'm just hiding out. Any news on Jon yet?"

"The manhunt rages on in full force. We do have a glimmer of good news though. The agent that was shot on duty in the command post may live. They have him in a drug induced coma while they are trying to minimize the swelling of his brain. The doctors are somewhat optimistic that he will live and have most of his brain functions intact.

"He was sitting at the computer bank when Jon walked in and would have been facing the door. Jon would have shot him first because he was in the position to send an alarm. Because he had to put down three more people before they could return fire, he may have rushed that first shot. The agent, seeing Jon shoot at him, may have been in the act of flinging himself backwards. Whatever the scenario the shot struck his forehead at an angle that caused the bullet to go upward exiting at the top of his head. The doctor that did the surgery thinks he has minimal brain damage and will have ninety percent recovery."

"That's great; he will be able to identify Jon."

"I don't know. I asked the doctor about it and he was very evasive. He said that until he had a chance to see what parts of the brain weren't functioning he couldn't tell me much. He might not be able to recognize faces or he might not be able to remember the incident at all. We just have to wait and see."

"Well, at least he is going to live. That alone is good news."

"We are all encouraged about that. He's a really nice guy with a family. What I called about is the watchers have asked that you spend as little time on deck as possible after dark. They are equipped with the best night scopes money can buy, but they don't want to shoot you by mistake. They are afraid that if you suddenly had an urge to move around on deck in the dark, an accident could occur."

"You don't have to tell me twice. I will not stick my head out of the cabin after the sun has gone down until I leave in the morning at five fifteen. I don't want them to shoot me by mistake either."

"Very good thinking. I'll talk to you later. Good night."

By him signing off with a good night, I suspected he was on the East coast. It was only four o'clock here. I was glad about a survivor, but it didn't offset the ten who didn't survive.

I had a clip-on light that I had rigged to light the cockpit. I discovered on my first trip with several people that when you were anchored in a cove on one of the offshore islands, it was convenient to have light in the cockpit. If you were trying to cook on the small barbeque that fit into a socket on the rail or even just serving food from the galley, it was not easy in the dark. I went out and clipped the light to my mainsail boom and coiled the extension cord next to the hatch. If I did need to go on deck for some reason, I could open the hatch wide enough to reach the cord and plug it in before going out. It wasn't very bright, but it would give enough light for anyone to plainly see me; plus by turning on the light, they would be warned I was coming out.

I opened my condition book one more time. With this rate of distractions, the condition book would be out of date before I could get through it. With no more calls interrupting me, I was able to spend a couple of hours going through the book. It was a good book for me; there were races for every one of my horses. It was as if I had handed in a list of the races I needed and the racing secretary had written all of them. You were normally pleased if you found more than half of the races you wanted. This was a rare book.

After I finished marking my races, I made a little supper for myself and tried to read. I couldn't keep my eyes open and finally put the book away and went to bed.

When I arrived at the barn in the morning, I was glad to see that no irate trainer waiting for me. All of the workers from the day before checked out good, and the morning went smoothly. Everyone was in a pleasant mood after an afternoon off and was looking forward to another one. When training was over, I hooked up my trailer and went to Pomona to pick up my filly.

I hardly recognized her. She had gained seventy-five or eighty pounds and had shed her rough coat. She was slick and shiny and looked like a different horse. She came out of her stall with a spring in her step and was bright eyed and taking an interest in life again. Her feet had grown out and looked great. He had done a terrific job with her. We got her loaded without mishap, and I brought her back to the barn with a little more confidence that she might make a race horse.

He said she had been going through the gate every morning, and since she had already started, I didn't need a gate card for her. I would give her a few days to get used to the new track surface and give her a try.

On the way to the boat I stopped to do some grocery shopping and stocked up for a couple of weeks. I didn't know how long I might need to hide out but felt sure it would be more than a week. I had to make three trips from the truck to the boat to get all of the junk I had bought aboard. By the time I put it all away. I decided I had enough for three weeks. I sat down to take a break and grabbed a Dr. Pepper and opened a bag of Oreo cookies. When I realized I had eaten half of the bag, I remembered why I don't buy them very often—I can't stop eating them once I start.

It was still early and I was a little restless. I considered walking across the street to have a drink but discarded it as a bad idea. If I ran into someone I knew, it might make a very awkward situation. If they expected to come back to the boat with me, I wouldn't be able to explain why I couldn't have company right now. It was best that I stayed where I was.

I called two of my owners, each of whom had a horse that we had not been able to find a race for, to let them know there was finally one in the book. Of course you can never get away with a brief conversation when you call an owner, and this was no exception. The two calls took more than an hour, and I was thinking there must be an easier way to notify owners about their horses.

I picked up the book I had tried to start last night, but my mind kept going over the last few days, and I couldn't get into the book. The racetrack grapevine is one of the most active and fastest information systems I have ever seen. I was truly amazed that there had not been one whisper about Jodi Breaux or her husband. It was possible that the FBI was still holding Jodi, but I doubted it. I would ask the next time I talked to Goodman. There was no way the newspaper could have mentioned either one of them because the FBI couldn't prove it was Jon at this point. I just thought someone would have had some inkling of Jodi being picked up by the FBI and would be asking questions. Not one whisper.

I eventually put the book aside and went to bed. I awoke in the morning and made my own breakfast again. I was already thinking ahead to the day in front of me as I ate. I was going to walk the filly I had just brought over. She had just worked and didn't need to go to the track, and I wanted to give her time to check out her new surroundings.

Santa Anita is equipped with walking machines throughout the barns. You rent them by the month and you have the option of taking an entire machine or renting just an arm or two and sharing it with another trainer. I had a whole machine, but it really wasn't enough during the busy time of the morning. I had to walk a few by hand and usually reserved this for the horses that played too much on the machine. A horse that liked to play around was a danger to himself and other horses on the machine. I had one horse, for example, that would pull the machine and get it going so fast all of the horses were in a gallop. Another type you had to be afraid of was the horse that would leap in the air, because if they caught a front leg over the lead line, they could bow a tendon. All of the lines came equipped with quick releases, but it still took a minute for someone to get to the machine and release the horse.

I decided to hand walk the filly the first day just to be on the safe side. They had the same machines at Pomona, and I was sure she was used to it; but I was taking into account that she was in a strange place with strange people and horses. There was no point in giving her a chance to hurt herself.

The morning went about normal and we finished by eleven. I had three to enter and stopped in the racing office to make the entries before coming back to the barn. I saw by the size of our muck pile that the stalls had all been seriously dirty today. This was a pretty clear indication that the grooms had not done much to them on the two dark days. They picked the bad spots and spread fresh straw over them to make them appear cleaned. This would happen on dark days if you didn't keep an eye on them because they wanted to get away early. I would have to give Gene his first talking. He knew better and may have left early himself.

I went back for the draw with an interest in seeing if the agents had anything to say about Jodi. Between them, the agents covered every barn on the track. If anyone on the track had any knowledge of the events, it would be one of the agents. The only mention of Jodi was one of the agents asking how her horse had run in Chicago on Sunday. When one of the other agents replied, "A bad third." There was not another mention of her. It felt strange to know something no one else knew.

When I returned to the barn, most of the help had left for the day. I had one horse in, and he was in the last race. I couldn't face sitting around all afternoon waiting for the last race and decided to go to a movie. I told James that I had something to do and if I didn't get back in time to run the horse.

In the afternoons there are never more than a dozen or so people at the movies so you can sit about anywhere you want. I took a seat in the last row so no one would be behind me and moved my holster from the back to the front. I was a little paranoid about sitting in the darkened theater, but no one was near me, and I had the comfort of my pistol. When the movie was over, I waited until everyone had cleared out before I left my seat. I remember thinking that it must be hell to be a fugitive and think every person you see or meet is looking for you.

I had plenty of time to make it back to the track for my race but couldn't work up the interest in going. I started for the boat but had only gone a few blocks before I changed my mind.

I didn't expect the horse to run very well in this spot and didn't want the owner to think the bad race was because I hadn't been there. I went to the track and made it with an hour to spare.

James had assumed I wasn't coming back and had already set up to run the horse. He seemed a little disappointed that I had made it back so I told him to go ahead and run him. I met him in the saddling paddock, just so my appearance was visible, in case the owner had come to watch his race. The horse lost a photo for fourth and didn't get a check but actually ran better than I had expected.

I stopped to talk to a friend, and by the time I got back to the barn, they had given him a bath and had him on the walker. I couldn't think of any reason I needed to hang around and headed for the boat. The traffic was murderous at that time of day, and it took me an hour and a half to make the marina. I thought about stopping to eat but decided I needed something to do with myself when I got on the boat. I hadn't had much luck trying to read.

As I was walking down the dock to my boat, the gentleman that has the boat on the other side of the dock came out to meet me. Our boats sit bow to bow and he had been there since I put my boat here a couple of years ago. I didn't know him very well since he had a power boat and sailors and power boaters don't have very much in common. They can't travel together because of the differences in speed and just kind of leave each other alone.

He said, "Hey Chance, were you supposed to meet someone here today."

"Not that I know of. Why?"

"A guy was here acting like he was waiting for you. He hung around about an hour before he finally left."

"What did he look like?"

"He was about six feet tall and weighed maybe one ninety. He had a week's growth of beard so I couldn't see his face very well. He was wearing a ball cap and I couldn't tell how much hair he had but what I could see around the cap was blond."

"I can't think of who that would be. Did you talk to him?"

"Just for a minute. My wife and I are taking a couple to Catalina this weekend. We hadn't been on the boat for about a month and thought we should come down and see what we needed in the way of supplies. We were sitting on the bridge having a martini when he came down. He didn't go aboard, but he walked all around the boat several times. He was pacing as if he was waiting for you and I didn't want to butt into your business. He walked down to the end of the dock and stood looking up the channel for a while. When he came back, he sat down on your dock storage box, and I asked him if I could help him. He asked me if I had seen you today, and when I said I hadn't seen you in a month or two he left."

"I have no idea who it could have been but thanks for letting me know. Have a good trip this weekend."

"Thank you."

I went aboard and locked myself in. I had a good idea who it was and I wasn't happy to realize he was back in town. It didn't make sense that he would still be in the country much less back here. I called Goodman and got his voice mail. I left a message, "This is Chance and I had a visitor this afternoon that answers the description of our guy. Call me as soon as you get this message."

I didn't know what else to do. Goodman had never given me a number to call if he wasn't available. I would have to wait until I heard from him, but I was not a happy camper.

I checked my watch every hour only to find it had only been five or ten minutes since I checked it last time. The first time or two I was sure my watch had stopped but finally had to admit it was my brain that had stopped. I sat on my bunk with my gun in my hand and thought how ironic it would be if I shot myself by accident. I would lay it down, only to snatch it back up every time my rigging creaked. This was insane; after all he was only a man. On the other hand, I wasn't the equivalent of ten FBI agents, and he handled them pretty easily.

When my cell phone rang, I must have jumped a foot off the bunk. I snatched up the phone thinking if it wasn't Goodman I would kill him the next time I saw him.

Goodman's voice was too calm as he said, "Hi Chance, what's up?"

I related the story my neighbor had told me, including the description, and waited for him to tell me everything would be alright.

Instead he said, "That doesn't sound like Jon. He is not six feet tall and doesn't weigh one ninety."

"When you're up on a flying bridge looking down, you can't distinguish between five ten or five eleven and six feet. If you weigh one sixty or one seventy and you have body armor on under your shirt, you could easily look one ninety. I have no doubt it was him. Very few people even know I own this boat, and most of them that do are female. Not one man who knows about my boat comes even close to matching that description."

He was silent for a long while thinking it over before he said, "You know what? Your instincts have been right every time so far. I am going to go out on a limb and advise my people that he has been seen locally. This area will be hit by a very expensive whirlwind. If he shows up tomorrow in Paris, France, I will be asking you for a job as a groom."

"Trust me when I tell you this is him."

"OK, you've sold me. I'll set the wheels in motion. Sit tight where you are. I'll put the watchers on alert and they will step up their surveillance. If he has come all this way to get you, he is as crazy as a run-over dog. I believe you that it's him. I just can't fathom his motive for being here."

"I can think of several reasons he would come here. He could have come back to pick up money or passports. He could have come here thinking this was the safest place in the country, since this would be the last place you would expect him to be. He could have come back thinking the detective agency would get him out of the country. He may have seen how tight the borders were closed and didn't know where else to go. It could be a combination of all of those things."

"Were you a bad person in another life? You think like one."

"I hope not, because I am too much of a wuss to be successful as a bad guy."

"Let me get off the phone and raise an alarm. We may get lucky now that we know he is here."

"I'll talk to you later. Good night."

Even after I had convinced him it was Jon, he didn't seem nearly as excited as I thought he would be. Maybe he wasn't really convinced and was just saying what he thought I wanted to hear. If he didn't take me serious about this, I was in big trouble. I had no doubt it was Jon, and if they didn't give me the protection I had been promised, I would have to protect myself. I wasn't sure how to go about that, but I would give it serious thought starting right now.

It wasn't dark yet and I made a bite to eat while I could see without lights. I had already decided that I would show no lights. If he hadn't seen me come aboard, I wasn't going to advertise that I was here. I lay on my bunk fully clothed and fell asleep sometime during the night. When the alarm went off, it scared me awake. I changed clothes in the dark and left in a hurry. I hoped the watchers knew it was me. I didn't want to be the victim of an accident.

I stopped for breakfast and arrived at the track without incident. Everything seemed so dully normal at the track that it seemed unreal. I kept looking at people and thinking, how can they be so complacent when the world is on the brink of disaster? Of course it wasn't their world that was on the brink, just my world.

I took my place in the grandstand and spent more time focusing my binoculars on the crowd than watching my horses. I told myself that this is not the place he would pick to come after me. He would want more privacy than here. I believed that, but nevertheless I kept looking through the crowd. I did watch the new filly for the entire time she was on the track. She didn't seem to be bothered by her new surroundings and galloped like a veteran.

I made my two entries and checked in at the barn. The filly had walked on the machine and had no problems. I could think of her as an older horse from here on. She didn't need any special care or handling.

I was thinking the morning was going well when one of the grooms stomped into my office obviously angry about something. I leaned back in my chair and said, "OK, Henry, get it off your chest before you blow a gasket."

"I want to know why Pug picks up an extra horse before I do. I've been down to three horses for six weeks. He's only been down to three for a week. It's not fair and I want to know why he got the horse?"

"Let me explain something to you, Henry. This is a maiden filly that has had several starts and never gotten a check. You don't want her. She is just extra work and isn't going to make you any money. If you still think she should be in your string, I will let you have her right now."

He shuffled from one foot to the other thinking it over and finally said, "You could have told me that in the beginning."

"Henry, you always get the best horses in the barn and make more win money than anyone here. Why would you suddenly think I was trying to jerk you around?"

"Well, she looks awfully good for a bad maiden. How was I supposed to know?"

After he walked out, I wondered for the millionth time if training was worth the effort. The horses were the easy part. The people would drive you nuts if you let them. Eleven people made up my permanent crew, and I doubt that a day passed without some kind of squabble between at least two of them. This was the problem that came up the most. Since the groom rubbing a horse that wins a race gets a bonus, there is constant bickering about who should be rubbing which horses. Some trainers split all of the bonuses among all of the grooms so they don't fight over who gets the better horses. I tried that one year and it didn't work. I found that the overall work ethic fell way off. There was no reason to keep your horses perfect if it wasn't going to make you any more money. They did as little as they could get by with.

I went over for the draw and had just walked in when I got a real shock. One of the agents was saying to another, "You will never guess who came by my house last night wanting to borrow five hundred dollars."

"That could be anyone of these dead beats. How would I ever guess which one?"

"It was Jon Miller."

"How did he know where you live?"

"When he and Jodi first came to town, my wife had them over for drinks. She thought it was the neighborly thing to do, but it didn't take. We never heard from them again."

"Did you loan him the money?"

"I had a bad day at the races and I only had about three fifty on me, but I let him have that."

"Did he say what he needed it for?"

"He claimed he and Jodi had a fight and he had stormed out without his wallet. He said when the bank opened this morning he would pay me back."

The conversation moved on to something else and I slipped out the door and went outside to find a place where I could call Goodman without being overheard. When he answered the phone, I plunged right in with, "Something is terribly wrong. Jon stopped by one of the agent's house last night trying to borrow five hundred dollars. What do you make of that?"

"Are you sure this is on the level?"

"I'm positive it's on the level."

"Did he give him the money?"

"He only had three fifty on him, but he gave him what he had."

A long silence followed before he said, "That is very interesting. We just discovered this morning that the LAPD has a body in the morgue of one of the vice presidents of Triple M detective agency. He was shot twice with a silenced twenty-two.

He was discovered two days ago, but it took a while for the paperwork to process through and get picked up by our office. It would appear that Jon's employers are trying to distance themselves from him, and whoever brought him the news got two twenty-two slugs as his reward. If they have left him out in the cold, I would suspect they have plans to silence him. We are not the only problem Jon is facing.

"What is interesting is that Jon is playing hide and seek with no funds. As well as everything has been planed up till now, I find it hard to believe that he didn't have escape funds readily available. It makes me wonder if they had started to suspect we had Jon tagged and were thinking this was his last job. If that is the case, I don't know how Anders fits into this picture. He might be the one that had decided it was time for Jon to retire. Who knows with people like them?"

"I just thought you would like to know he has no money."

"I wanted very much to know that, and thanks for calling. It takes away a lot of his options and will make our job much easier. It cost big money to extract yourself from the middle of a nation-wide manhunt without getting caught. Without that money he has to depend on getting lucky, and that is iffy at best."

"Just out of curiosity what is the status of Jodi Breaux? She hasn't shown up at the track. Are you guys holding her?"

"No, we released her, and she has gone to New York to stay with her mother. We didn't have anything to hold her on, and we don't think she had a clue about what was going on. We still have Anders in custody, but if something doesn't turn up soon, we may have to release him also."

"We are getting ready for the draw and I should go. I'll talk to you later."

I didn't have time to mull over the conversation because the draw was underway when I returned to the racing office. I got both of my horses in with good positions and went to the barn feeling good about things.

I had a horse in the fifth race today that belonged to me, and I told James to run him for me. I knew James liked playing trainer. He enjoyed running the horses and wanted the experience. I didn't feel the need to do it just for the experience and would rather let him do it when I could. I didn't want owners mad that I wasn't running their horse, so I couldn't let him run them unless I just couldn't make it, but the ones that belonged to me were my call.

I went straight to the boat and intended to spend the afternoon calling owners. As I came down the walkway, I noticed a new boat tied up at the end of the dock. It was a sixty- or seventy-foot beauty. None of the slips were large enough for boats that size and so they saved the ends of the docks for them. This one was flying a Mexican flag and was probably just a transient stopping for a day or two. I didn't see anyone aboard and assumed they had all gone ashore.

I had lunch and settled down with my phone and the paperwork on the horses. I found that I had to have my training schedule in hand when I called owners, because for some reason they asked for specifics on things like dates and times of their works. These things didn't mean anything to most of them, but I guess they wanted me to think they were really on top of the training on every horse. Every now and then I would throw in a bogus time just to test them and never got a reaction. I did that today with an owner that was getting on my nerves. I told him his horse had gone five-eighths in one sixteen flat, and that it was the fourth fastest time of the day. I can run that fast, and anyone that knew anything at all would recognize that I had made a mistake in the time. He never said a word and just kept asking questions.

I had finished my last call when my phone rang. It was Goodman and he said, "Things are really heating up. We had a court hearing this morning and the judge set bail for Anders. When we released him, he went directly to a bank. When he came out, he stood on the sidewalk for a second as if he was undecided about what to do next, and someone took that opportunity to shoot him right between the eyes. It was a heavy caliber rifle and it took the back of his head off. Someone is erasing their trail with gusto. We didn't have enough to charge him and two high-priced attorneys showed up demanding his release. They wanted him out of our hands as quickly as possible. They expected him to go to the bank and had it staked out waiting for him. We are back to playing catch up, with them always a step ahead of us.

"We inquired about his visit to the bank, and it turned out he had come in to withdraw money. When they informed him the account had been closed, he was very upset and demanded to know when and by whom. The bank told us the same thing they told him. It was done by wire yesterday, and whoever did it had all of the passwords to authorize the withdrawal. They had no way of knowing who was on the other end of the transaction, but it came from Germany."

"They obviously have more than one assassin on their payroll. You may be mistaken by thinking you are looking for only one."

"We don't think so. We think they left Anders in jail just long enough to import a shooter before they had him released. Two men on the Homeland Security watch list arrived at LAX and left again after only one day in town. We think they were brought in to take care of Anders. Homeland Security didn't share that information with us until after the fact."

"All I can say is wow. These people aren't stand up kind of guys. I wouldn't want to work for them. That might explain why Jon seems to be adrift. Any word on Jon?"

"Not yet, but we are turning over every leaf and every rock. He can't stay here very long before we wrap him up. We would love to take him alive since he is our last link to his employers. The detective agency is shuttered and a moving van cleaned out the building a couple of days ago. We have been trying to bring some of the employees in for questioning, but they have all faded into the woodwork. The only people we have located are a couple of low-level secretaries who didn't do anything but answer phones and mail letters. They know less than we do."

"When you say faded into the woodwork, do you mean they are hiding from you, or they have left the country?"

"We are starting to believe they may have left the country. All of their homes show signs of hasty abandonment, and not a single one of them has shown up on the radar anywhere."

"This is starting to sound like an episode of Spy versus Spy in Mad Comics. It's hard to believe that an organization like this can have existed in this country all of these years and never attracted any attention."

"We have been saying the same thing, among ourselves."

"Call me if anything develops. I'll talk to you later."

After I hung up, I sat thinking about what was going on. Anders must have known too much about the organization. They wouldn't need to kill him just because he had been exposed otherwise. It was scary that they would eliminate an important part of the company simply because the FBI thought he was a part of it. They didn't even wait to see how much the Bureau actually knew. Anders must have been much more important than an enforcer like Jon. If they would eliminate Anders so quickly, it was a good bet that Jon was certainly on their list.

That would explain why he had not been able to leave the country and why he appeared to have no money. They had withdrawn all support and were trying to force him to surface so they could get to him. The fact that Jon was still alive showed me that he was aware of his situation. I had to admit that deep down I was pulling for him. I guess it is just an ingrained trait to root for the underdog.

I made supper before dark and intended to show no lights again tonight. I was shocked to find out that Jon knew about my boat since I had taken such great pains to keep it a secret. Evidently one of those times that I thought someone was following, they actually were. Since he already knew about the boat, all I could do was hope he thought I wasn't on it. If he saw lights he would know I was there.

When I arrived at the barn in the morning, James handed me an envelope saying, "This was stuck in the office door when I got here this morning."

The envelope was sealed and said, Chance Holden, Personal. I went into the office away from prying eyes to open it. I had a premonition that it was from Jon.

The note read, Chance, I need to talk to one of your clients. Please have Robert Goodman call me at this number at three o'clock this afternoon. Tell him not to call early because I won't turn the phone on until three. John Miller.

I read the note twice, trying to feel the desperation of the man who wrote it. If he was reaching out to the FBI, it was obvious that he knew he was running out of options. I would have to wait until I got to the grandstand before I called Goodman. I was still taking no chances that anyone would ever find out I had any part in this.

As soon as I reached the grandstand, I called Goodman. When I read him the note, I heard him take a deep breath, but he was noncommittal about it to me. He wrote down the number and thanked me. End of conversation.

I sat and speculated about where Jon was trying to go with this approach, and what he was trying to achieve. In the end I had to admit to myself that I didn't have a clue what he was thinking. I would have to wait and see what developed from this contact.

I made my entries for the day and went to the barn. I had two horses in today, and since they belonged to owners, I would have to be here, but my mind was on everything except racehorses. The day dragged by at an agonizingly slow pace.

When three o'clock came and went, I was on pins and needles, hoping for a call from Goodman. I knew that was silly because Goodman was going to be busy acting on whatever Jon had to tell him. He wasn't going to have time to even think of me.

The races were over at last, and it hadn't been a complete flop. I had a second and a third for my efforts. I'd had a lot worse days in my career. The horse that ran third was the horse that I thought had the best chance to win his race. It just shows you how little you know.

I went straight to the boat, thinking I should be home in time to have supper before dark. I was sticking to my plan of showing no lights. The big boat was still on the end of the dock and I still saw no signs of life aboard.

I ate and cleaned up my dishes in the waning light. It was still light outside, but in the closed-up cabin, it was very dim.

I was a little restless, but I had no intentions of going outside. I didn't know what evils lurked out there and didn't want to find out. I finally fell asleep on my bunk fully clothed. It was getting to be a habit.

I was sound asleep when I was startled by all hell breaking loose on the dock. People were running up and down shouting at each other, and it sounded like a gang war was going on. I raised the corner of my curtain and peeked out. I could see a dozen high-beam lights all up and down the dock. People seemed to be crawling all over every boat and shining their lights everywhere. I couldn't make any sense of the whole thing. I raised my hatch enough to reach the extension cord and plugged my cockpit light in. I stood in the cockpit watching a bunch of insane people running all over the dock. While I was standing there, I could hear sirens and saw the approach of a dozen cars with flashing red lights. My first thought was someone had called the police to come and break up a riot, but when the first red lights arrived, the number of lights and people on the dock increased.

I could see a group of lights congregated on the dock right where the ramp joined the dock. I couldn't see what the lights were trained on because a dozen people were milling around whatever they were looking at. My boat was pretty far out on the dock, and the people crawling around the boats hadn't reached me yet. I couldn't decide whether I should walk down to see what was going on or just stay on my boat and wait. They were coming up the dock checking every boat and would reach me in ten minutes or so. After seeing them find someone on a boat up the way, I decided I would just wait right here. They weren't treating them very well at all. They had a group of three or four around them, shining their lights in the couple's faces, and you could see by the reaction of the pair they were scaring the hell out of them. Whatever the questions were about, the couple wasn't doing much beyond shaking their heads no.

They were within three or four boats of my slip when a gentleman came walking up the dock toward me. He wasn't in the light and I couldn't see him very well until he turned in at my slip. He was obviously coming to talk to me, and he was wearing a jacket with FBI written in large bright letters. He stopped alongside and said, "Mr. Holden, may I come aboard?"

"Of course."

He stepped up on the deck with enough caution that I knew he was not a boat person. I couldn't contain my curiosity any longer and asked, "What the hell is going on? I've never seen anything like this before."

"We have a little bit of a problem here that we need to discuss before these cops reach your boat. I need to ask you a serious question. Did you shoot him?"

"Shoot who? Did I shoot him? Hell no. I was locked in my cabin sound asleep. These people running around like chickens are policemen?"

"Most of them are LAPD. A few of our people are here, but they are looking for a different thing. The police haven't realized yet that the man was shot by a sniper and are questioning anyone that is in the area. When they reach us, I would appreciate your silence about any connection to the man who was shot and any connection to us. Until we have time to do a little investigating of what actually happened, we don't wish to be involved in a pissing contest with the police."

"My connection to the man who was shot? Is it Jon that was shot?"

"Yes, but at this time it is not at all clear who shot him. We had two snipers with him in their scopes, and they both have the same story. While they all had him in their sights, his head suddenly exploded. They both deny firing, and their rifles appear to be unfired. They heard no shot and saw no muzzle flash. We have no idea where the shot came from or who fired it."

At that instant three policemen turned in at my dock. Two of them were shining lights on my boat while the third one was shining his light in my face. I was sitting directly under a light and don't know why he felt a need for the light in my face. One of the men looking over my boat leaped up on the deck, and judging by the sound of the clunk, he was wearing boots or very heavy shoes.

I opened my mouth without thinking as usual, "Hey schmuck, be careful with those clodhoppers on my deck."

I now had two flashlight beams in my face. He came toward me stomping hard on the deck with each step to show his defiance. "I'm not kidding. I didn't invite you aboard, and if you don't cut that shit out you're going swimming. I will throw your ass overboard."

"The guy standing alongside on the dock must have foreseen this was about to get out of hand. He said, "OK John, knock it off. Get off the guy's boat."

John said, "I'm going to wait for him to try and throw me off."

John had not only pissed me off, he had now stepped on his buddies toes, and he raised his voice several notches. "I said get off his boat, now."

John took his time about making up his mind what he was going to do, and his buddy said again. "Now."

John clambered down making as much contact with the deck and side of the boat as he could. His buddy said, "Go help Jake with the search."

"I'm not finished here yet."

"I've had all of your smart mouth I can put up with today. You go pick up your partner and go back on patrol. If you say one more word or stand there like your thinking about saying one more word, I'll have you on report in the morning. As many black marks as you already have, that might get you a vacation."

John wheeled around and stomped away.

The officer standing on the dock had moved the light out of my face and his tone was apologetic as he said, "Do you know anything about this, sir."

"Not a thing. I was asleep until I heard people running up and down the dock."

"Did you hear a gun shot?"

"No sir, just some people running around the dock."

"Do you own this boat?"

"Yes sir."

"Have you docked it here long?"

"A little over two years."

"What do you do for a living?"

"I train racehorses."

"Do you know this gentleman?" he pointed at the FBI agent.

"No sir, he saw me standing in the cockpit watching and came over to explain what was going on."

"OK, if anyone comes over to question you, tell them Sergeant Banks already talked to you."

"OK, goodnight."

As he walked away, the agent said, "That was too easy."

"I think he was embarrassed by his associate."

"He should have been, but it was still too easy," he put out his hand as he said, "My name's Fred Castle by the way."

"Glad to meet you; you seem to know who I am."

"If they come back, give them the same amount of information you just gave him. Until we know what went on here, we don't need LAPD stomping all over this case."

As he walked away, the thought crossed my mind that they must have a factory somewhere that produced these agents. He was so similar to Goodman they could have been relatives. I looked at my watch for the first time since I woke up and saw that it was three o'clock. It would take so long to go back to sleep that it didn't make sense to even try. I saw them wheeling a gurney up the ramp and assumed it was the body. It had been at least an hour since this started and that seemed like a long time to leave the body lying on the dock.

I went in and turned the lights on in the cabin. I didn't need to hide anymore—at least not from Jon. I made a really big breakfast of bacon and eggs with pancakes. I don't like coffee and always get funny looks when people see me having Dr. Pepper with breakfast. That's where I get my caffeine.

I took my time eating and waited to see if I would get another visit from the police. Mr. Castle didn't seem to think they had questioned me enough. It didn't matter to me if they came back or not. I didn't know anything about the shooting and not very much about anything else.

The feelings I had were mixed and hard to describe. I was both relieved that it was over and sad at the way it ended. I was scared to think he had been coming for me and gratified that the FBI had provided the protection they had promised me. Jon had been the worst kind of monster, and no one should feel bad about him dying. Still, I had empathy for a man suddenly turned on by the people he thought were his friends and allies. He had nowhere to turn, and all of the escape paths had closed for him with no warning. He was trapped by the betrayal of his own kind and in the end didn't even know why. The only good thing you could say about it was the end came quickly—he probable never even knew it happened. The worst part is no one would ever have to answer for it. Goodman had led me to believe that if Jon died, there would little or no chance of making a connection to anyone.

I cleaned up after my breakfast and changed clothes. I walked up the dock toward the ramp, most of which the police had blocked with yellow tape. I could barely squeeze by to reach the ramp. They had left a police officer on duty to ensure no one messed with the tape, and he watched me very carefully as I went by. I was still a little early but what the hell. I went on to the track. It wasn't as if the track wouldn't be open. Even in the dark, some trainers would already have horses on the track.

I was very lethargic all morning. I couldn't concentrate on the simplest of tasks. I just kept thinking that if I had known how this would end, I would never have started with it. Then I would follow that thought by thinking it had to end this way or someway very similar. I just hadn't allowed myself to think it through to the end. I probably was trying to avoid facing what the end would have to be.

Sometime in mid-morning I received a call from St. Germaine. That alarmed me for a second because he had never called before. He wanted to give me a message from Goodman, who was busy. They didn't want me to enter their horse again until they talked to me. I had been expecting as much and wasn't surprised. When we talked they would probably ask me to sell him for them. If they didn't want a big profit over what they had paid for him, I would buy him myself, just to get them out quick and easy. The horse was worth the money and I liked him.

I would have gone to my apartment except I had left part of my paperwork on the boat and had to go back for it. As I came down the ramp, I saw the yellow tape and the cop were still there. I noticed that the big boat on the end of the dock had pulled out, but what I really noticed was that someone was sitting on my dock box waiting for me. When I got close enough to recognize the horse's ass from last night, I almost turned around and went back to my truck.

He heard me coming down the dock and shifted around to face me. He was staring at me with his best Clint Eastwood imitation as I walked up. "To what do I owe this pleasure," I said.

"I thought I would search your boat in the daylight while I can really see it."

"OK, where's your warrant?"

"I don't need a warrant to go aboard this boat. This is a crime scene."

"No it isn't. The crime scene is way down at the other end of the dock. Do you see any yellow tape around here? You need a warrant to get on this boat if you don't want to go swimming."

"Listen, tough guy. In case you haven't noticed, I'm wearing a gun."

"That's alright; so am I."

He had just opened his mouth to say something cool when it registered on him what I had said. The calm way I had said it left no doubt in his mind that I was armed, and he now began to worry about who I really might be. I had been having a quiet conversation with an FBI agent when they had walked up, and I had shown no fear of him when he tried to intimidate me. It was beginning to dawn on him for the first time that maybe I was someone he should leave alone.

He made one last try by saying, "You better have a permit for the weapon."

"I do, and it's probably better than yours."

That clinched it in his mind, and now he was looking for a way to withdraw gracefully. He said, "If I had more time I would insist you let me on that boat, but it's my day off, and I have things to do. You can bet I'll be back"

"That's fine, come back anytime. Just don't forget the warrant."

He swaggered off down the dock, and I had the feeling I had seen him for the last time. I hoped so at least. Guys like him are a pain in the butt.

I went aboard and got my paperwork as well as a few things that I wanted to take home with me. I locked everything down and went back to my apartment. I could get back to using the boat for pleasure instead of a hideout.

I was cleaning my apartment and getting things shipshape when my cell phone rang. I hoped it was Goodman and it was. "Are you at your apartment?"

"Yes."

"If you are going to be there for awhile, I would like to come by."

"I'm in for the night. Come on by."

"See you in a little bit."

I had finished cleaning and settled down with a beer when he knocked on the door. He came in and sat down as if he was tired to the bone. He declined my offer of a beer and said, "I'm sure you're dying of curiosity."

"That's an understatement."

"I'll do my best to answer your questions, but a lot of this is guesswork."

"My first question is, what did you and Jon talk about when you called him?"

"He was willing to give us everything he knew, but he asked for more than I could give him in return. He wanted total immunity. It wasn't possible to give him that when we knew he had at least a dozen murders on his hands. I told him the best I could offer was no death penalty. He said no thanks and hung up. He was using a burn phone, and that was the first call made on it, so by the time we had any kind of a location, he was long gone."

"Do you have any idea why he was coming after me?"

"That will take a little explaining. We don't think he was coming for you. We don't think he even knew you were on the boat. In going through all of the transcripts of the recordings we had made of Jon's cell phone calls, we found a call from Anders in which he discussed you. Anders must have asked him to check you out because they had found out that I was a client of yours and because I was one of the agents on the task force that was checking them out. They needed to know if you were involved. Jon told Anders that he didn't think you knew anything about the investigation and wasn't of any interest to them. He said something in jest that turned out to not be a total joke. He told Anders that you owned a nice little seaworthy sailboat, and if he ever needed to get out of the country, he would steal it and sail away. We think he was coming to steal your boat. The bag he had with him was mostly clothes, and they were the kind you would take on a boat trip."

"That is amazing. Mr. Castle said your people didn't fire the shot that killed him. Do you know yet who did?"

"That is where we are totally guessing, but here is what we think. The call from Anders that I just told you about was made from the detective agency. We suspect that all of the calls to and from the agency were recorded, and someone going through those recordings took more heed of Jon's statement about your boat than we did. We think that when they started the search for Jon, they put someone in place to watch your boat. When Jon showed up at the dock the other day, they assumed he was casing the boat with the intentions of stealing it, and they put an assassin in place to take him if he showed up there again."

"Do you have any idea where the shot came from?"

"We have a pretty good idea. The thing that put us off track was the damage that was done by the shot. We first thought it was a fifty caliber sniper rifle. With a trained sniper, that rifle has good accuracy at a mile or more. The shot could have been fired from one of the hotels across the channel. In the autopsy this morning, which I was observing when St. Germaine called you, we discovered that it was a much smaller rifle with an exploding bullet. We started looking for a much closer position for the shooter. We came to the conclusion that the shooter was most likely aboard the boat tied at the end of your dock. We tried to get a judge to issue a search warrant, but he refused to sign it on the grounds we didn't have probable cause and were just fishing. It didn't make much difference anyway because by that time the boat had left the dock and put to sea. We contacted the coast guard to see if they could board the boat and search it for us. By the time they located the boat, it had already reached international waters and since it was foreign owned, they declined to board her.

The boat was registered to the governor of Sonora Mexico, and when they arrived they had specifically asked to be berthed on your dock. When they had checked the boats on your dock after the shooting, the boat was locked down tight and no one appeared to be aboard. If we had known it was a smaller caliber rifle, we would have paid a lot more attention at the time. Being registered to the governor of a Mexican state may have made the boat off limits to us anyway."

"That explains how, but I don't understand why they killed them."

"You have to keep in mind that Anders had been deeply involved with these people for a long time. He had been at bank headquarters for a dozen years with the title of head of security. He knew all of the players and what role they played. I don't think they were aware that he was involving himself in Jon's hits. That would be like sending a general with a head full of top secret information to the front line as a spotter for a sniper. It's something you are not knowingly going to allow. When we arrested him, his fate was sealed. They would have moved heaven and earth to get him out of our hands. He knew enough to bring them down and they couldn't take any chances.

"That explains Anders, but why Jon"

"I think they killed Jon because they were afraid of what he might do in retaliation for their killing of Anders. He was a very capable individual, and in their place I would have been frightened too. If they hadn't felt forced to kill Anders, they would probably have let Jon just disappear. Anders was killed to protect their company, and Jon was killed to protect their lives."

"So what do you do now?"

"We are finished with this task force. We don't have anything further to pursue. St. Germaine and I will be assigned to another detail. They plan to leave a couple of people to monitor the activities of the Dutch bank in hopes of something turning up down the road, but everyone else will be reassigned."

"What you are telling me is the people behind this whole thing are home free?"

"Basically that's true. We set out to close down an assassin, and that's what we did. Our operation was successful, but we would like to have taken it much deeper. The problem is that we are talking about a foreign corporation that we have no authority to investigate. We will turn over the case file that we have on the bank to Interpol, but most of our information is circumstantial so they don't have a lot to work with. They will have an idea of where to look if something similar occurs in the future. Other than that we haven't done the bank much harm."

"What do you want me to do about your horse?"

"I almost forgot," he said as he reached in his jacket pocket, "I have something for you."

He handed me an envelope and waited for me to open it without giving me a clue as to what it contained. It contained a notarized bill of sale for the horse signed by him and St. Germaine.

"You don't need to do that. I'm willing to buy the horse from you."

"That would open a can of worms that we wouldn't like. We already have a problem with the money he earned in his two races. We went racing to find an assassin, and that money was budgeted as an expense. We have almost all of our money back, and the department heads are concerned about a red flag when the auditors see that on our expense account. That money was allocated as an expense, and is already written off. If we showed a profit, it would be impossible for our accounting department to reconcile it, and if we tried to sell the horse, it would be impossible to put a price on him. By the time all of the people who would have to sign off on a sale finished fighting over what would be a proper price, the horse would have died of old age...Plus the cost of his upkeep while this lengthy debate takes place might add up to more than the horse's potential sale price. Everyone agrees this is the best way to handle the disposal of the horse. We all wish you good luck with him."

"What should I do about my gun permit?"

"We discussed that also. The consensus was that you should keep that for the time being. We can't be positive they won't send someone after you, but we see no reason why they should. It would be foolish of them to come after you just in case you might know something, but to cover the very small chance it could happen, we will leave you the gun permit. It has no expiration date and will be good until someday in the future some low-grade paper pusher asks why a horse trainer in California has a permit, and revokes it. They would notify you if that should occur."

"If you run into James Wadell, give him my regards. I guess you know he's my ex-wife's uncle."

He smiled as he said, "Yeah, I knew that. I run into him much too often. He's my boss."

I laughed as I said, "I'm glad I didn't know that. I might have worried that he was trying to get me killed."

"Chance, it has been great meeting you and working with you. I wish things could have ended on a more positive note." he said as he got to his feet. "William and I wish you all of the best. He would have come with me tonight, but they have already sent him on to Seattle to set up our new office space. You have my cell phone number, and if you have any suspicions that anything is out of line, don't hesitate to call me. I'll have someone check it out right away. We are going to leave one watcher on your apartment for a week, but we don't expect you will be bothered." He put out his hand, and I shook it and walked him to the door.

As the door closed behind him I knew it was really over.